by Michael Maxwell Steer

Book 1

The ColourMuse Company

© 1999-2007 v9.3

design Sam Steer
'designosaurs' © Clancy Steer

http://colourmuse.org
Maxwell Steer, 125 Duck St, Tisbury SP3 6LJ

Welcome to ColourMuse

Younger Readers ...

If you're like others I've taught over the last few years your progress will take off like a rocket with coloured notes. Many of these tunes were composed by people of *your* age. **Why not see if you could compose one?** Then visit our website and upload it. **We're also interested in your favourite music.** Join the ColourMuse Club and tell us what you like.

Older Readers ...

With coloured notes all age-groups can read music immediately. Having taught beginners for many years using black notation, I've noticed the dramatic difference in progress with coloured notation.

Beginners usually find time values easy enough because the note/tail shapes are reasonably distinct, but many have a lot of difficulty learning pitch from black notes. A great number, including very bright students, find it hard to see lines and spaces as *next-door* notes. With coloured noteheads you simply play the correct colour and *hey presto!*

Recent research has shown this is because the brain processes colour in a separate area, and thus the colour recognition bypasses the complex decoding required for monochrome data when everything is the same colour. That having been said, there remains an advantage in having the lines present from the beginning 'as part of the furniture' so that the appearance of the printed page doesn't alter when the student progresses to black notation.

From observing the difference in young children's responses to black and coloured notation I conclude that what we generally call dyslexia is almost a normal condition in under-8s. The difficulty in decoding a set of monochrome symbols links, I believe, to difficulties most beginners have with addressing a specifc hand or finger. I've come to suppose that this may be a perfectly normal stage in the brain's development, whereby reading difficulties are another reflexion of a child learning to prioritise stimuli. By reducing the density of black information for beginners the whole process of brain-hand coordination seems to develop faster. Even with able children coloured notes accelerate the prioritsation of both visual and 'handed' information much faster than black.

This may *appear* a random selection of music – and in a way it is – but I've road-tested this method for 10 years, discarding every piece that doesn't seem to pass muster with kids. I believe that the goal of teaching is to create a virtuous circle where pupils' enjoyment of what they're playing feeds back directly into enthusiasm and faster progress. Each piece offers a carefully graduated step up the scale (ladder) of self-confidence. It would normally take 6-9 months for a beginner to work throu this book. To make learning even easier, every page displays commonly used symbols.

I'm mindful that beginners today are born into a completely different world. These volumes address the consciousness of children whose outlook is formed by the cultural assumptions of mass market music. Much as we may wish to work towards expanding their cultural horizons I've found this is the surest way to start.

Good luck.

Maxwell

On our website ...

You'll find the latest information about ColourMuse – including video demonstrations of all these pieces by **Harry Jeffrey** which can be viewed on the web or downloaded.

Visit the Colour-Muse Club to see what other young composers have wrttien and upload your own music.

There's lots of news – be sure to find it first at http://colourmuse.org

On the CD ...

Track listing

ColourMuse CD1

01 *Tuning C* – Use this to test if your piano is at concert pitch
02 01.1 *My first tunes*
03 01.2
04 01.3
05 02.1 with count
06 02.1 without count
07 02.2
08 02.3 slow
09 02.3 fast
10 03.1 *C Major*
11 03.2 RH
12 03.2 LH

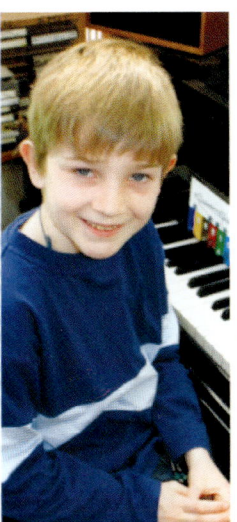

13 03.2 HT
14 03.3
15 04.1 *A mountain*
16 04.2
17 05 RH
18 05 LH
19 05 HT
20 05.4
21 06.1
22 06.2
23 07.1 with count
24 07.1 without count
25 07.2
26 07.3 slow
27 07.3 fast
28 08.1 slow
29 08.2 slow
30 08.2 fast
31 09.1 *Quavers*
32 09.2
33 10 *Shanty*
34 *C scale*
35 11.1 *Little Donkey*
36 11.2
37 12 *A Minor*
38 13 *Skipping* intro
39 13
40 *G Scale*
41 14.2 *Frère Jacques*
42 15.1 *Jingle Bells* RH
43 15.1 LH
44 15.1 HT
44 15.2
46 16 *Night River*
47 17 *Semiquavers*

48 18 *Silent Night*
49 19.1 *JustB4T* intro
50 19.1 together
51 19.2
52 20.1 *The first*
53 20.2
54 21.1
55 21.1 *Steps* slow RH
56 21.1 fast RH
57 21.1 LH
56 21.1 HT
59 22.1 *Lavender's Blue* RH
60 22.1 LH
61 22.1 HT
62 22.2
63 22.3
64 23 *Can UB Sure?*
65 24 *Boogie* intro
66 24 with lyric
66 24 without lyric
68 24 accompaniment
69 25 *Circuit* intro
70 25 with lyric
71 25 without lyric
72 25 accompaniment
73 26 *Horseriding*
74 27 *Ashgrove* RH
75 27 LH
76 28 HT
77 28 *Double Decker*
78 29 *Happy Birthday*
79 30 *Lillibulero* RH
80 30 LH
81 30 HT

Welcome to ColourMuse Book 1

With coloured notes you can read and understand music from the first page.

Here are the colours we use –

There is a colour key chart to sit behind the keyboard, which matches the colours of the printed notes. And there are optional coloured stickers for each note as well.

Here's what the printed notes look like:

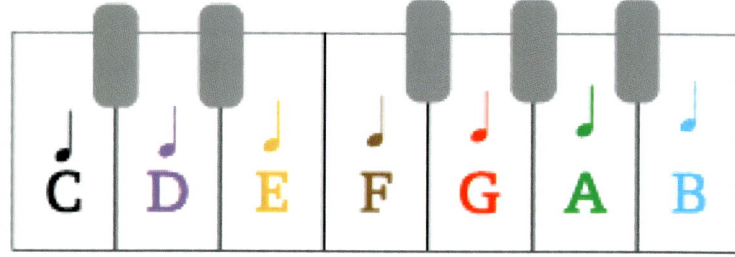

Notice ⟶ we use **lines** ... *and* ... **spaces** alternately.

This colour key chart shows where they are on the keyboard:

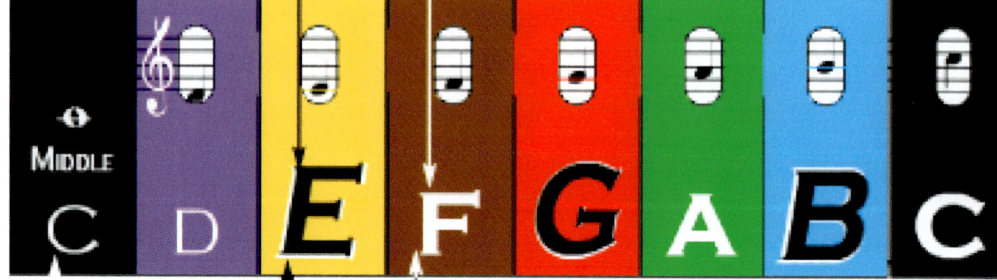

See how the big **black** letters correspond to the printed lines,
 ... while the big white letters match the notes on spaces.
The smaller white letters are the notes outside the 5 lines (known as a stave).

Note Lengths

Meet the family ...

Hi! My name's Charly –
Charly Crotchet
When I go for a walk
just keep in step with me.

Left, right, left right, left right ...

Each crotchet is 1 beat

And here's my Mum –
Mummy Minim
We *wait* a beat as
she waves to us.

One - *wait*

Each minim is 2 beats

At the end of the walk we meet
Granpa Semibreve
He's a bit slow, so we count
4 beats when we see him.

One, two, three, four, *off!*

Each semibreve is 4 beats

*There are reminders about
them on every page.*

Now let's go for a walk with them

1	2	3	4	1	2	3	4
My	name's	**Char-**	**ly,**	I'm	a	**Crot-**	**chet.**

1	2	3	4	1	2	3	4
Come	and	meet	my	**Mum**	(wait)	*Hi!*	*wa*

1	2	3	4	1	2	3	4	1	2	3	4
O-	ver	here's	my	**Gran-**	/	/	/	**pa.**	/		/

1	2	3	4	1	2	3	4
'Hi	(wait)	**Mum!'**	(wait)	'Hal-	lo	Char-	ly.

1	2	3	4	1	2	3	4	1	2	3	4
Lunch	is	read-	y	**Gran-**				**pa.**	/	/	/

Notes

○ Semi-breve — 4 beats

𝅗𝅥 Minim — 2 beats

♩ Crotchet — 1 beat

ColourMuse

6

Setting up the keyboard stickers

Notice that black notes come in groups of 3 & groups of 2

Look for the group of 2 in the <u>middle</u> of the keyboard

Middle C is the first note to the left of them.

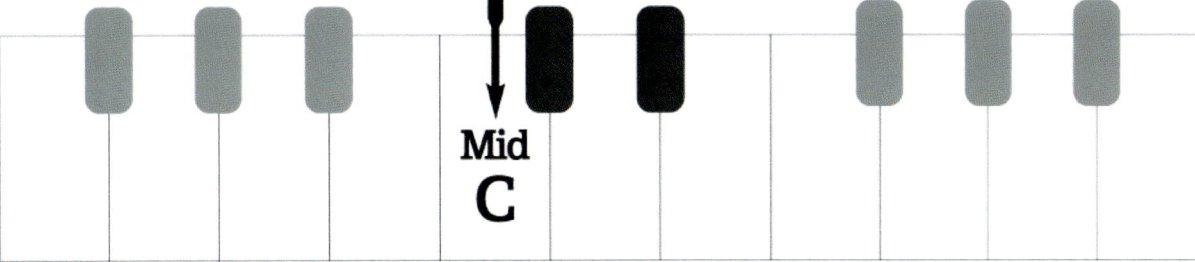

The colours should then appear like this

Place your hands on the keyboard with both thumbs qon Middle C. **Thumbs** are number 1 – numero uno.

Try to keep the knuckles level. Don't let the 'little' end of the hand fall over as it will make it harder for the fingers to work.

Notes

Semi-breve 4 beats

Minim 2 beats

Crotchet 1 beat

Let's get started at the keyboard

Put your **Right Hand** (RH) with the thumb on middle C

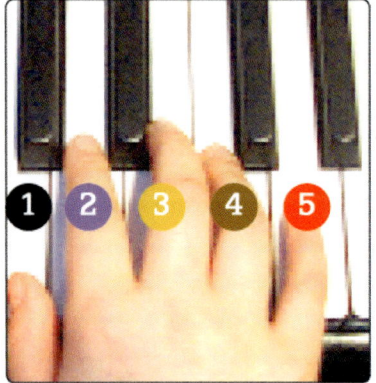

Then play up and down, starting with the thumb.
Look at how the coloured note-heads match the keys.

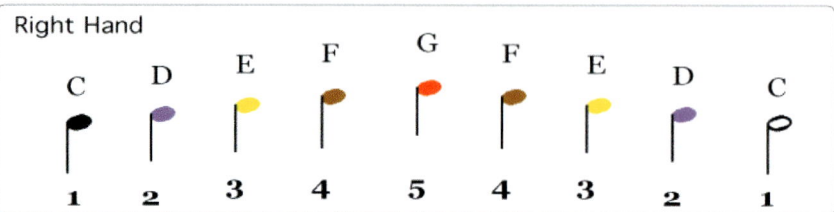

Now let's see what those notes look like when we put them on a *stave*.

The *stave* is what we call the **5 lines** music is written on ...

Each line and *each* space represents
 a separate note on the piano.

On each stave there is a **clef**, like this *Lollipop* 𝄞 (also called a **treble clef**)
 It tells us these notes belong to the *Right Hand* or <u>RH</u> for short.

Music is like walking: each step is called a beat.
 To make it easier to read, we divide the notes up into regular patterns
 called bars. These are indicated by **bar lines**.

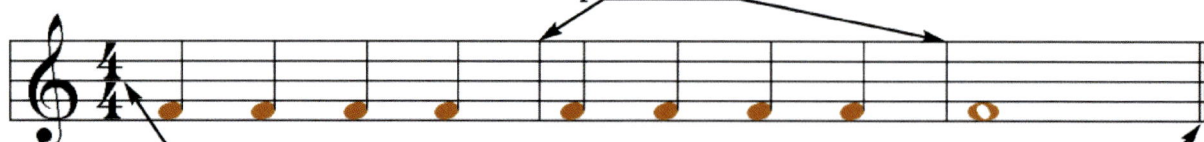

There's a Time Sign at the start telling us how many beats in a bar.
 And at the end there's a **<u>Double Bar</u>** telling us to stop.

How many 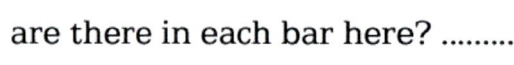 are there in each bar here? ....

Now we're ready to play from the notes ...
 Notice that there are slashes (/ / / /) written under the notes
 to show the crotchet beat and help you keep in time.

1 My first tunes

1a Going up & down stairs

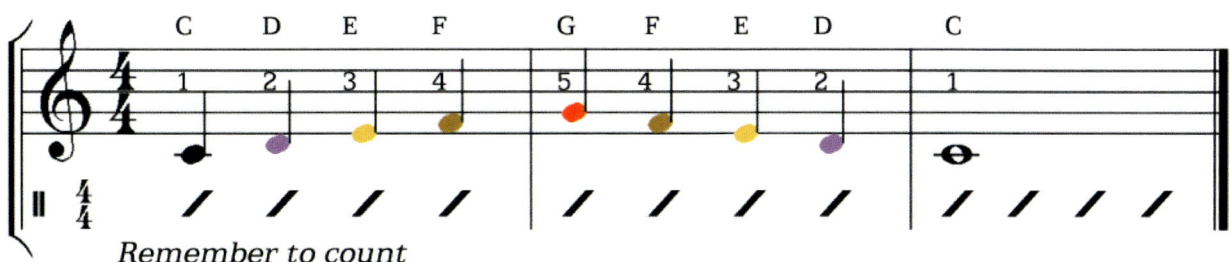

Remember to count

1b Going up an escalator - twice

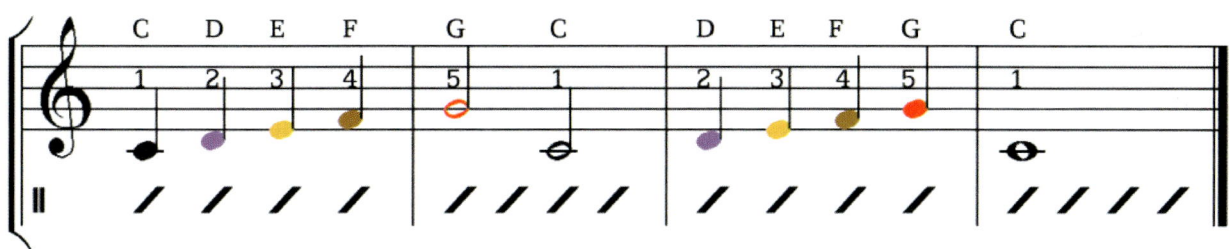

1c Where does the cow jump over the moon?

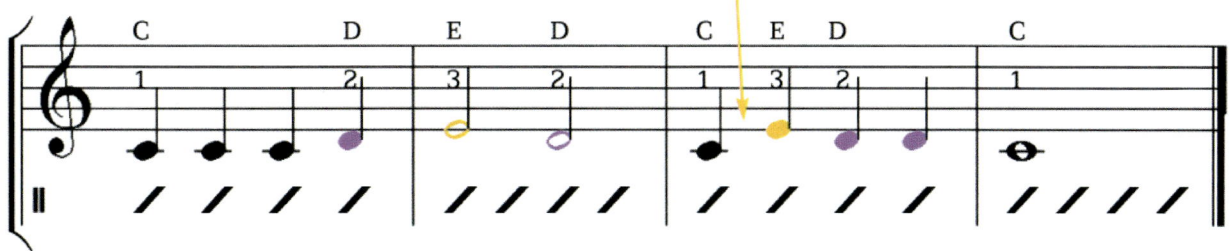

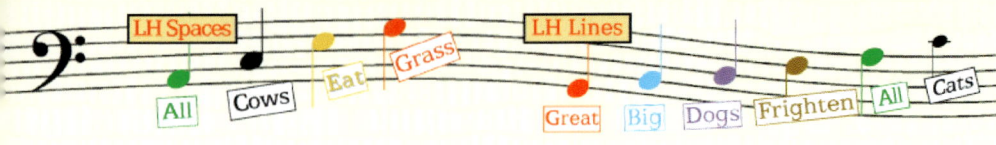

Notes

We're ready to play the Left Hand (LH)

This time, put your **Left Hand** (LH) thumb on middle C

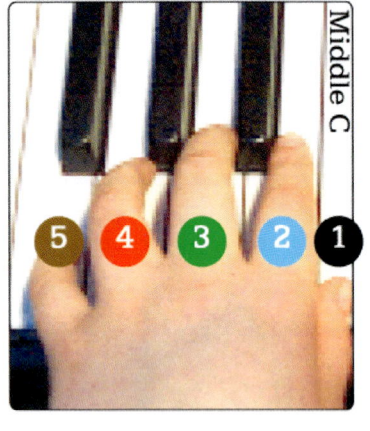

Now play *down* and *up*,
noting the 2 beat Minims

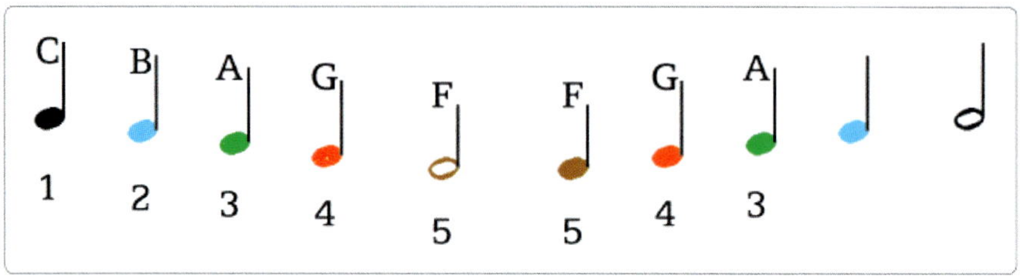

○
Semi-
breve
4 beats

So, let's meet the *Left Hand* sign – 𝄢 the **Snail** (also called the **bass clef**)

When both hands play the two clefs are bracketed together.

Notice that **Middle C is** doesn't belong to either stave.
It has its own line in the middle.

𝅗𝅥
Minim
2 beats

However, to make it easier to see

which hand should play **Middle C** we move it
nearer the <u>Lollipop</u> clef for the <u>Right Hand</u> (RH),
but nearer the <u>Snail</u> clef for the <u>Left Hand</u> (LH).

♩
Crotchet
1 beat

So let's see what happens when we play with
<u>Hands Together</u> (HT for short) ...

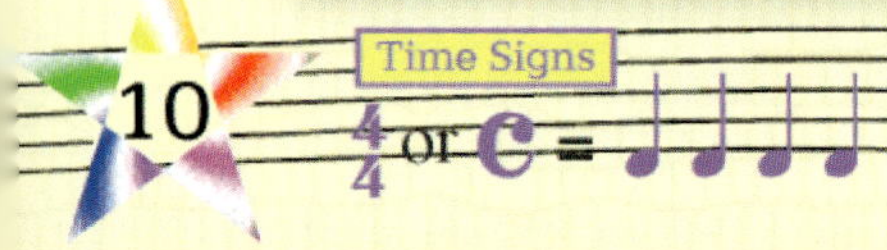

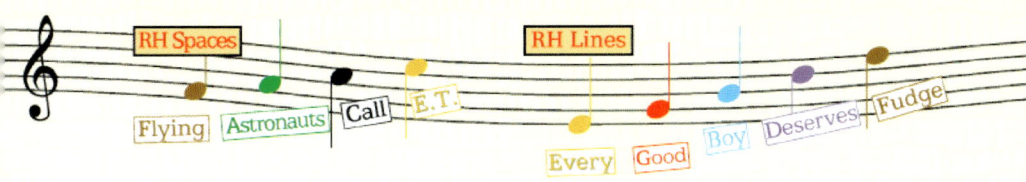

2 The Left Hand

2a See how easy it can be

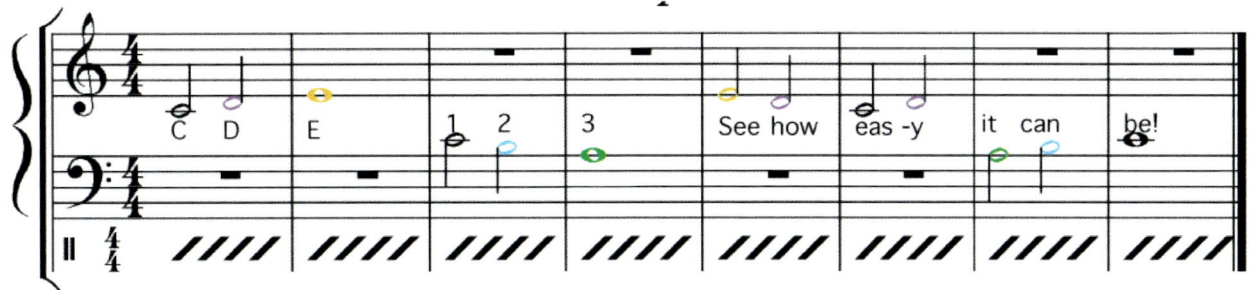

Remember to count

2b Running & stopping

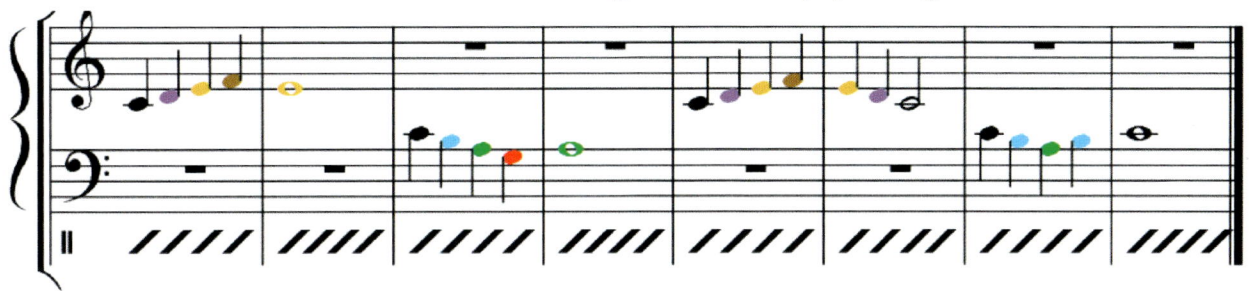

2c Simple Simon

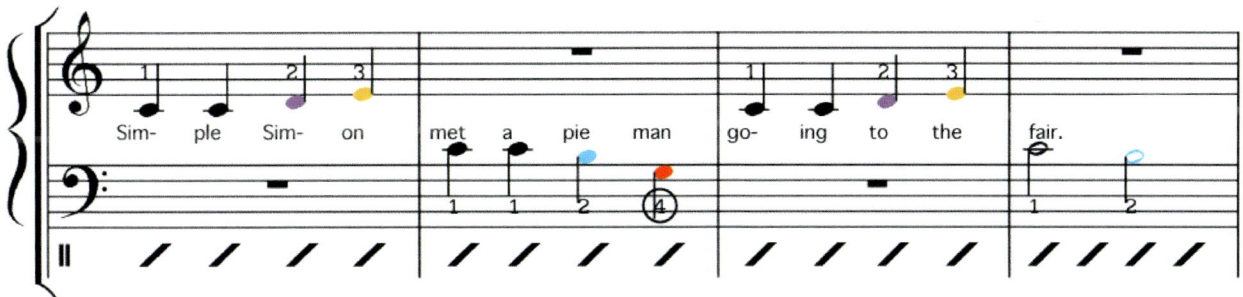

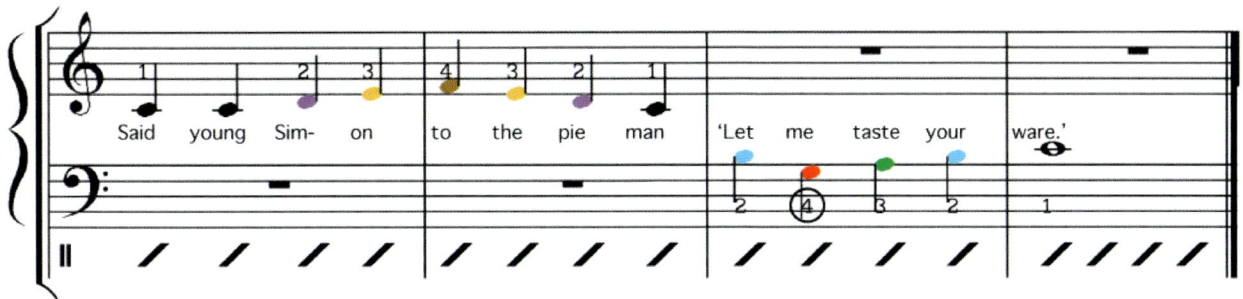

Write in their names

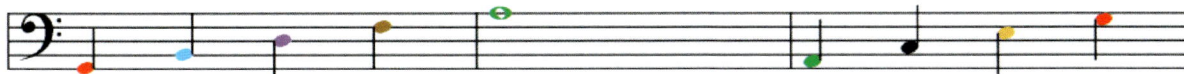

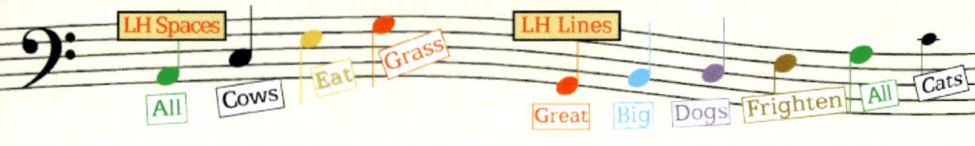

Notes

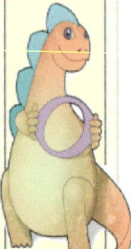

Semi-breve
4 beats

Scales

The way we move outward from the centre of the keyboard is by putting our thumb under our middle finger.

Try this now.
First play middle C with your thumb.
Then play D with your second;
and E with your third.
Now
slide your thumb under and continue until you reach the next with your little finger.

Congratulations. You've just played the Scale of C.
The word *scale* means the eight notes from C to C – or D to D, etc.
Another word for the eight notes from C to C (or D to D, etc) is an octave, from the latin *octo* = eight

Minim
2 beats

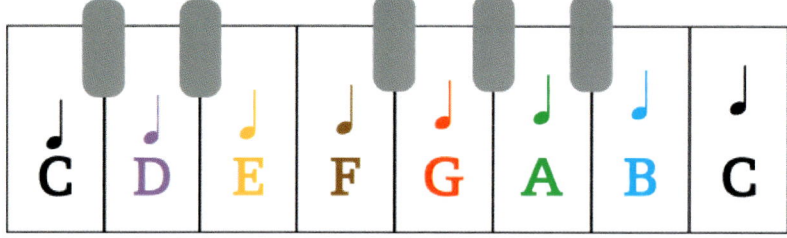

This is how it's notated.

Now put your little finger back on the C you finished on and come back to the middle: 5 - 4 - 3 - 2 - 1. *Then* do the thumb-passing maneuver in reverse,

Crotchet
1 beat

putting your *middle* finger over the top of your thumb.

Try it with the other thumb on middle C – going in the opposite direction.

When you've done that try using *both* hands, starting from middle C – mirroring out and back in.

What you've just played is the scale of C major, 'contrary motion' – that means hands going in the opposite directions.

Fingers in **circles** ① mean you *stretch a finger* or *change hand position*: Fingers in **boxes** ③ mean both hands *play the same finger*.

3 C Major

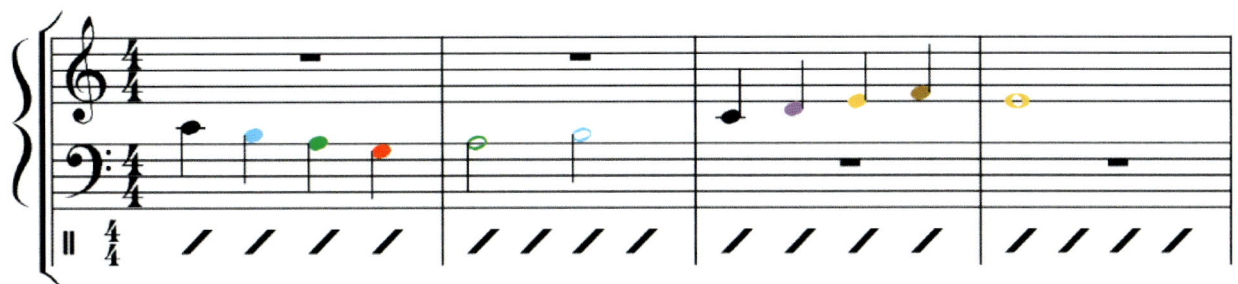

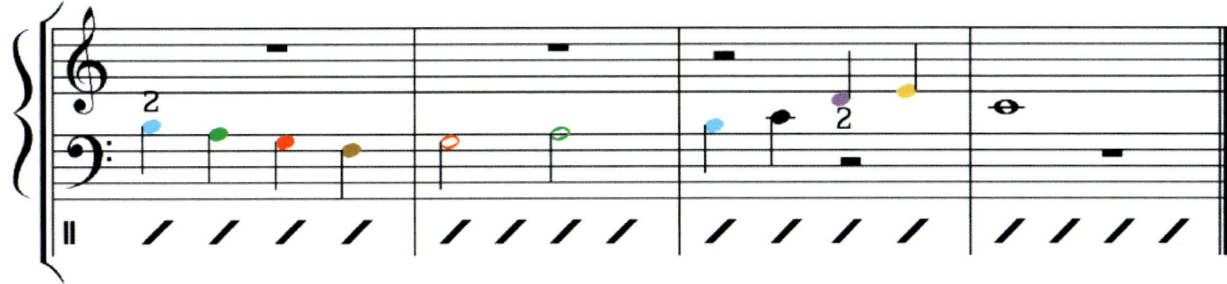

3b Scale of C Major

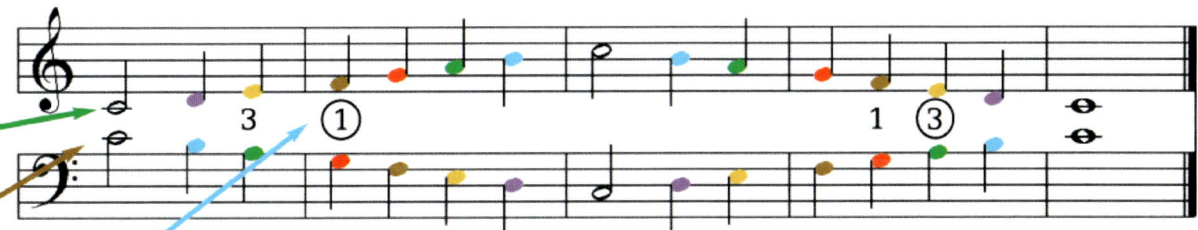

3c Climbing the highest hill

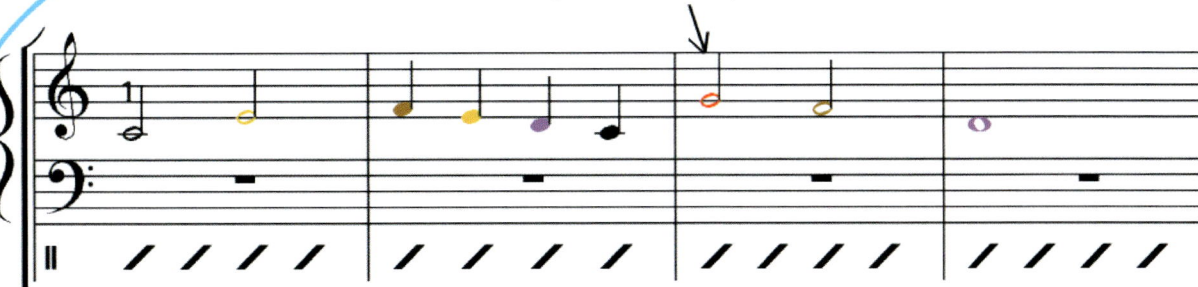

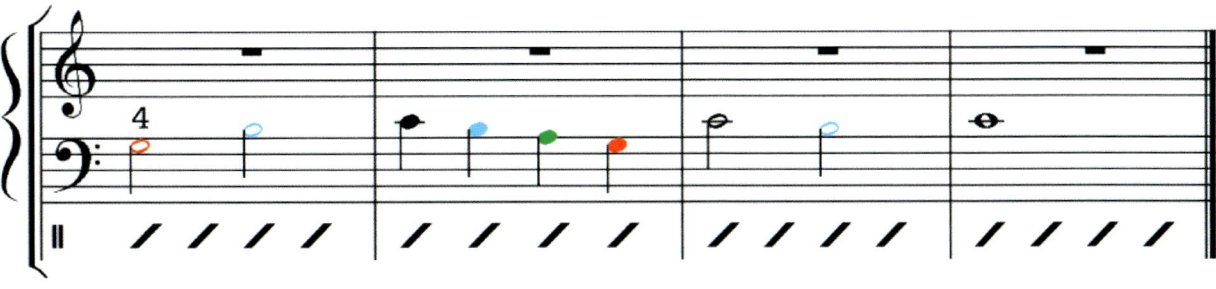

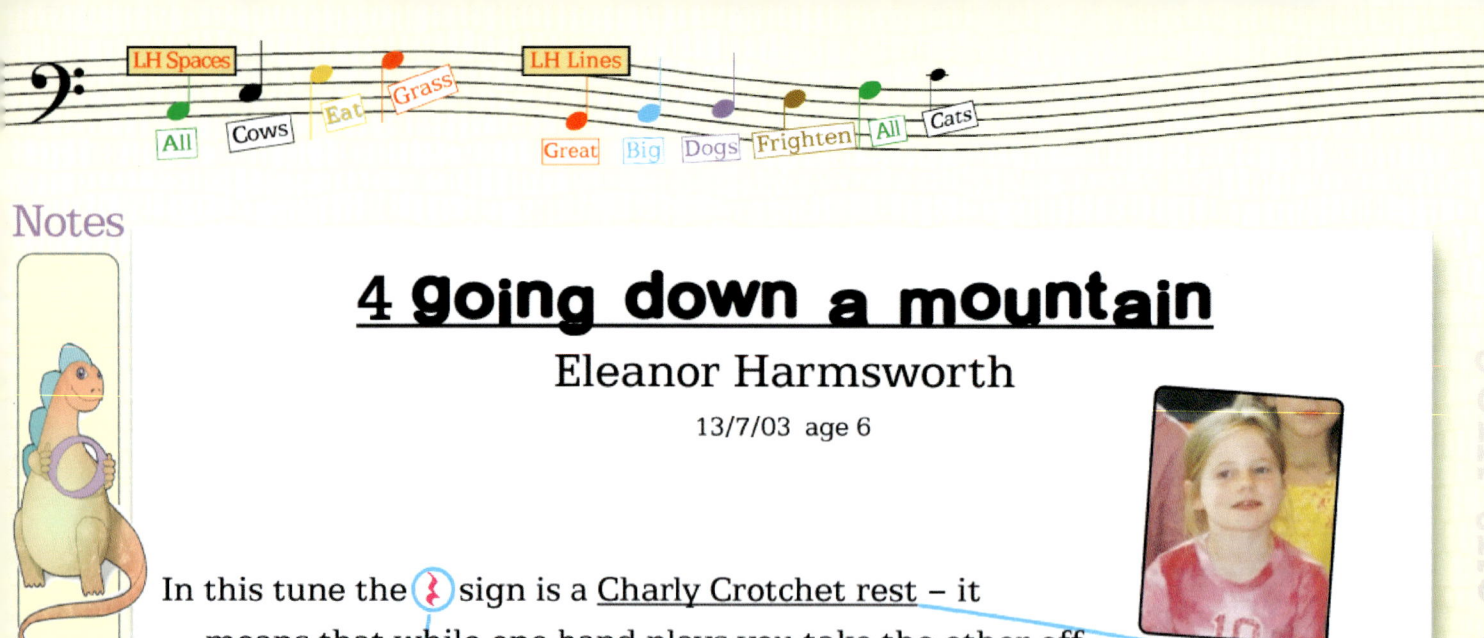

4 going down a mountain

Eleanor Harmsworth
13/7/03 age 6

In this tune the 𝄽 sign is a Charly Crotchet rest – it means that while one hand plays you take the other off.

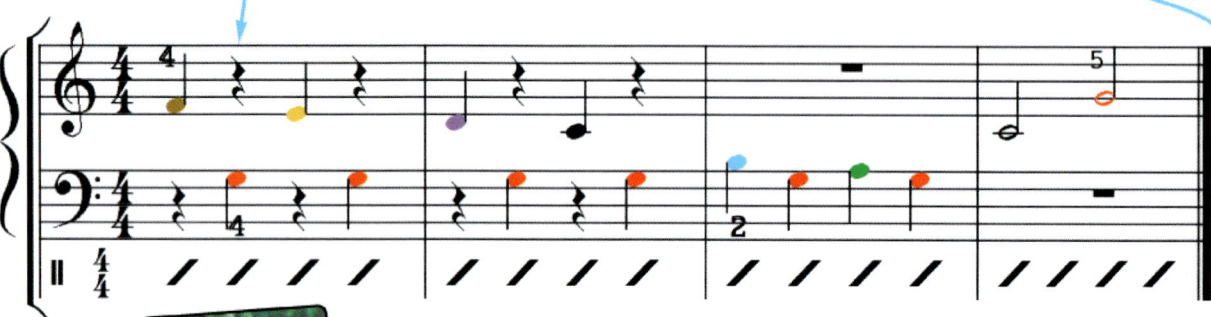

4b jumping
Georgina Foster
21/12/02 age 7

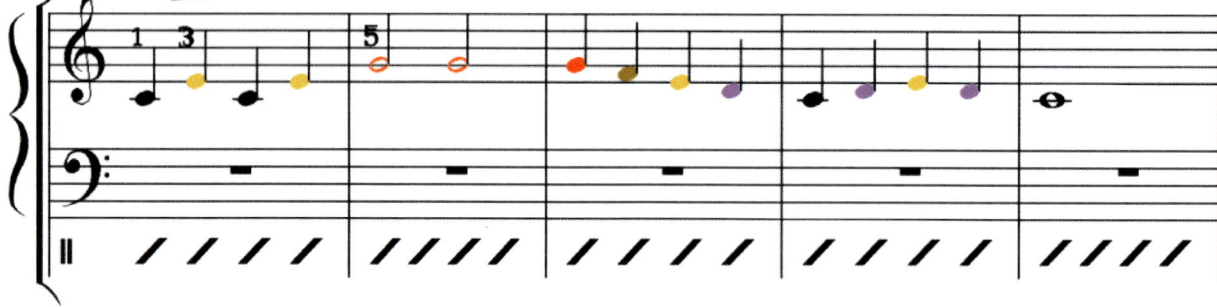

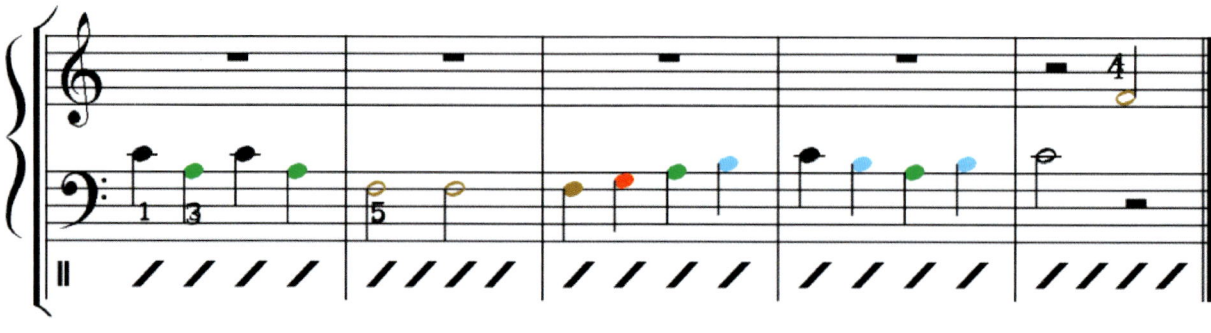

5 XPANDING

Play each hand separately ...

Boxes round the finger 1 mean that both hands play the same finger.

... then add them together

5b BITTY PIECE

Sarah Hewland

23/03/04 age 8

Halfway throu this piece the time changes from **3 beats** in a bar to **4 beats**

Join the fingers to make it sound smooth here

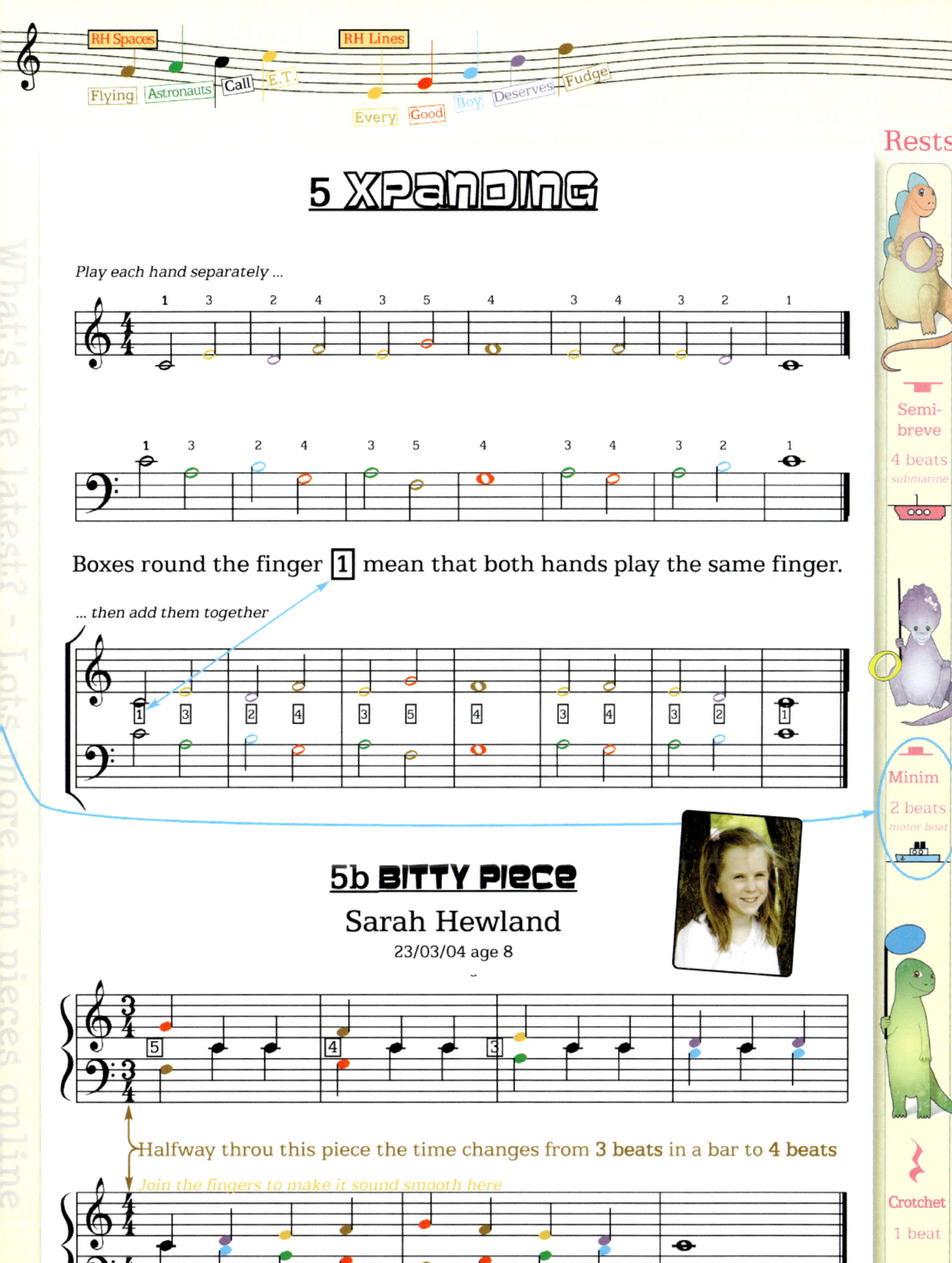

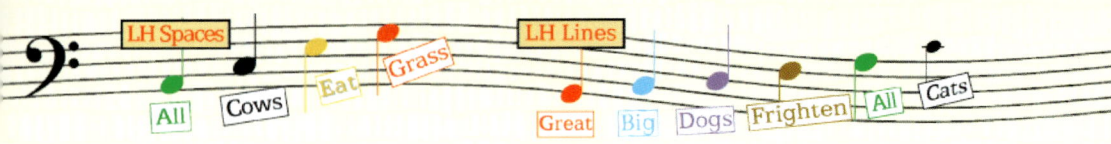

Notes

6a clair de lune

Notice in this piece how the LH in line 2 starts one note higher than middle C

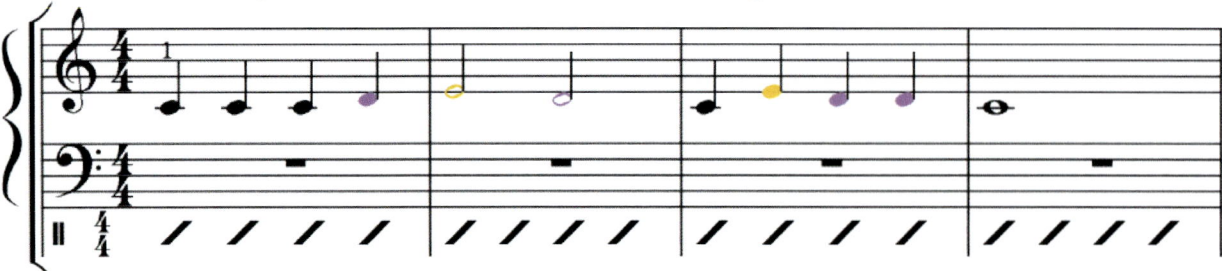

This is how purple D is written in the LH, it's the same note as the ones you've just played in the RH

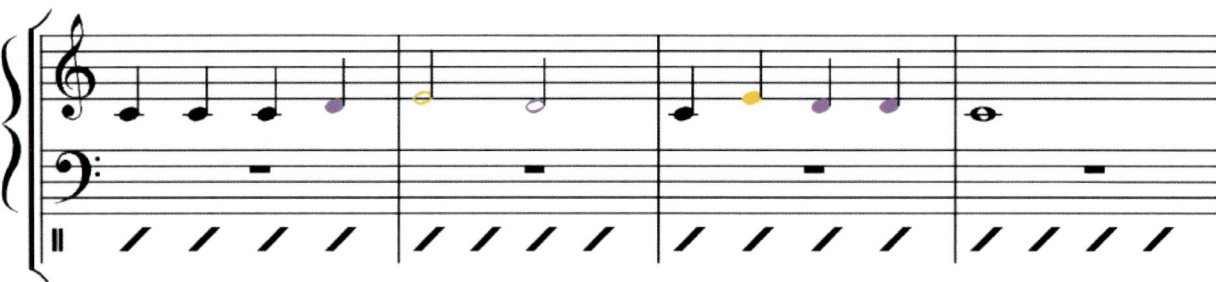

6b twinkle twinkle little star

Here it's the RH turn to move up one note

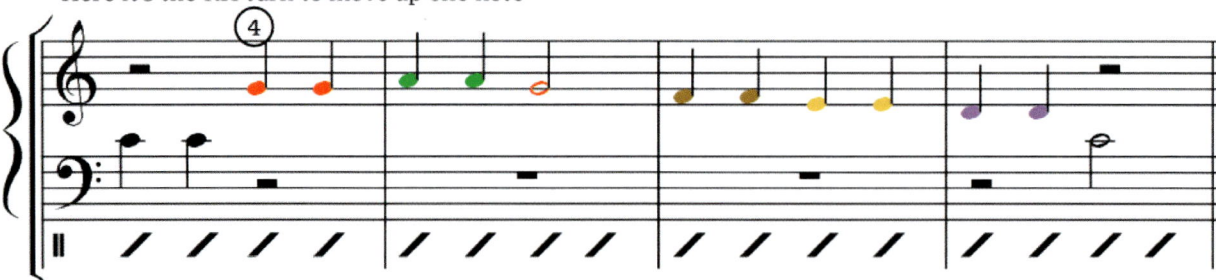

These signs mean you repeat the music

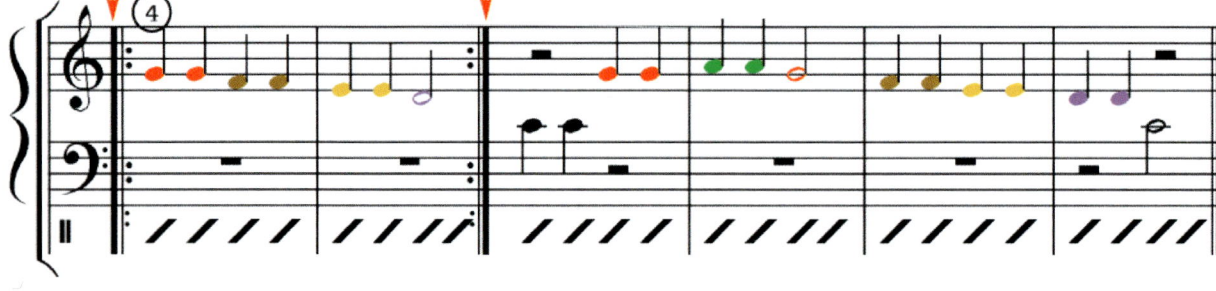

A few things it helps to know

Time Signs

So far, nearly all the pieces we have done have had 4 beats in a bar – written $\frac{4}{4}$
In fact 4 in a bar is so popular that the time sign is sometimes just written as
C (short for Common Time, not C major as people often think). *Turn to Tune 15 on p27 to see what it looks like.*

4 The 4 at the **top** means the **number** of beats:
4 The 4 at the **bottom** tells us the beats are **crotchets**.
3 But we also have pieces with **3 beats** in a bar: the 4 at the **bottom** reminds us the
4 beats are still **crotchets**. In the future we'll meet other time signs as well.

Rests

Take a moment to look at the rests on the RH side of the page. Notice how the
<u>Semibreve</u> rest (4 beats) at the top *hangs down* from the line, like a <u>submarine</u> *under* the water – while the <u>Minim</u> rest (2 beats) sits *on* the line, like a <u>motorboat</u>
Then there's the **Crotchet** rest (1 beat) which is just a squiggle.
Finally there is the **Quaver** rest, worth half a beat which we meet in 17 on p29.

Whole Steps & Half Steps

A **whole step** (or tone) is when you go from C to D. A **half step** (or semitone) is when you go from any white key to its nearest black neighbour. *Try playing these and listen to the difference.* If you play from E to F you can hear that this too is a half step? So is B to C. But the distance between all the other white notes is a whole step.

When we play C major scale the distance between the first three white keys are all **whole steps**, then comes a **half step**.

Each white and black piano key is the <u>same distance</u> apart. There are 12 of them in an octave.

But we only use 7 in the **major** scale. So there's a **standard pattern of whole steps & half-steps**, like this in every major scale.

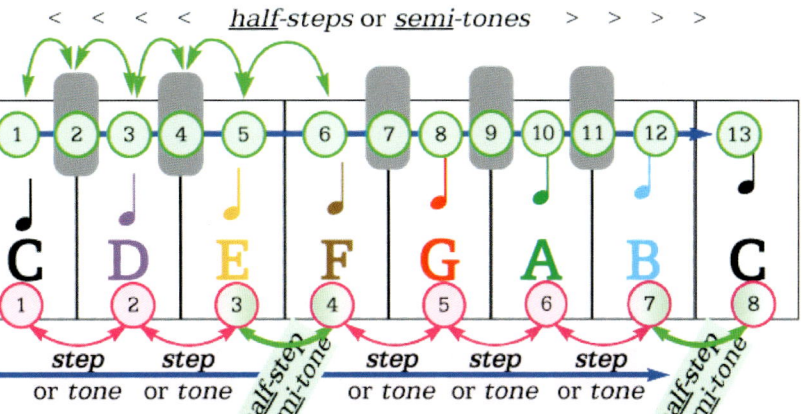

Note that the black keys don't have their own names. We call them by their nearest white note – so the black key *above* C, is called C# (*sharp*), or the black key *above* F is called F#. *But* we can also refer them as *flats*, so B♭ (flat) means the black key *below* B. This may seem a bit confusing at first, but you soon get the hang of it.

Rests

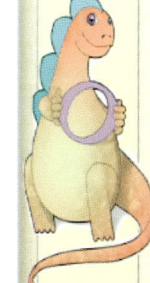

Semi-breve
4 beats
submarine

Minim
2 beats
motor boat

Crotchet
1 beat

17

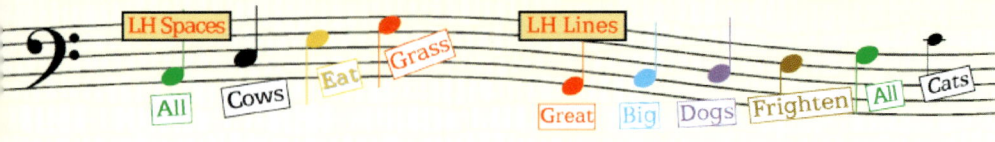

Notes

○ Semi-breve
4 beats

𝅗𝅥 Minim
2 beats

♩ Crotchet
1 beat

3 Beat Notes

This is a big moment.
    Let's remind ourselves of the family notes we already know ...

1 beat   2 beats   3 beats   4 beats

What's missing in the gap? **A 3 beat note.**

This is where we meet an important new rule:

A dot after a note makes it half as long again

So meet the newest member of the family: Aunty Dotty and her baby.
    Dotty is worth 2 beats, like Mum, and as half of two is one —
    2 + 1 = 3 — so Dotty & my new cousin together are worth **3 beats**.

Here's another way of looking at 3 beats

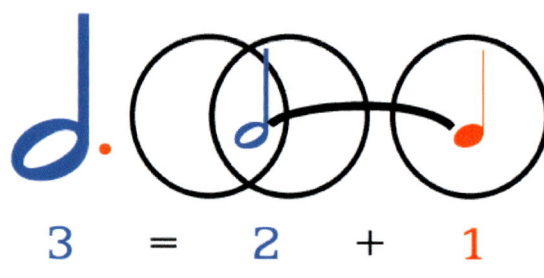

3 = 2 + 1

There's a reminder on the bottom of each page.

18

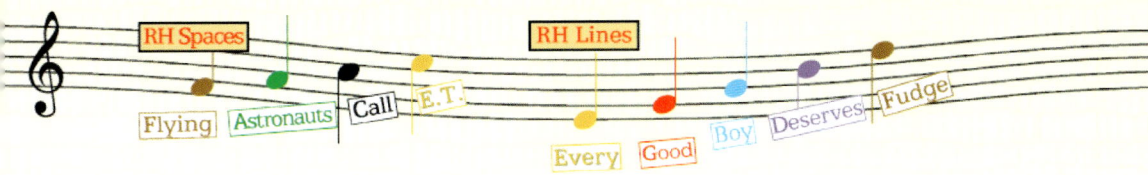

7a Swinging

A dot after a note makes it half as long again

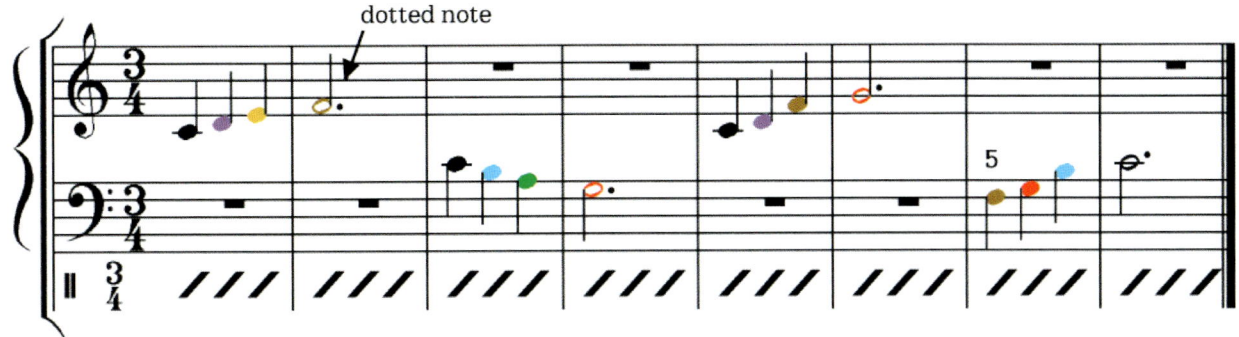

7b Wandering around

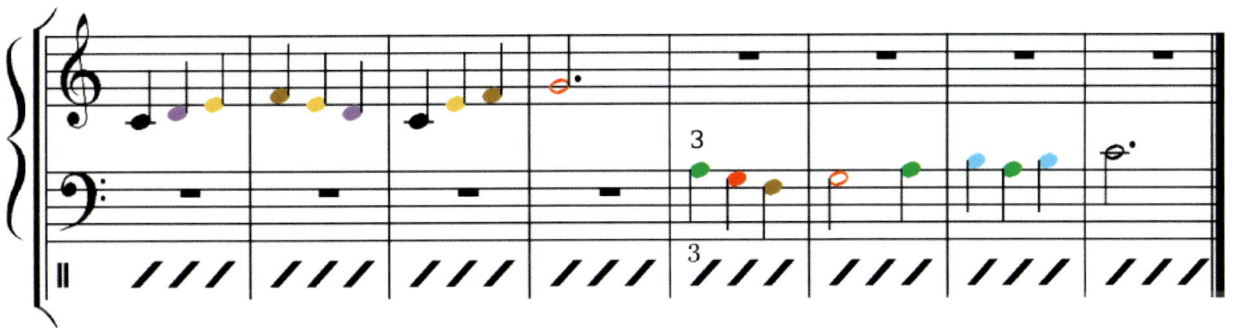

7c Together again

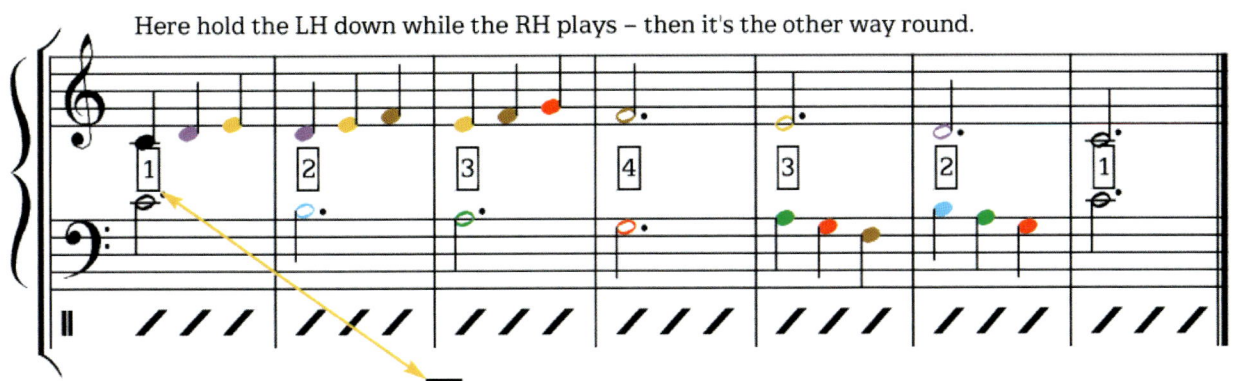

Boxes round the finger 1 mean that both hands play the same finger.

Notes

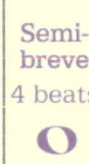
Semi-breve
4 beats

dotted Minim
3 beats

Minim
2 beats

Crotchet
1 beat

Quaver
½ beat

8 Quick Quavers

Now we're going to meet my little sister **Quilly the Quaver**. She always runs wherever she goes – she's *twice* as fast as me.

If you see **Quilly Quaver** by herself, she looks like this:  but sometimes she's hanging upside down from the banisters!

And sometimes she's with a friend. **2 Quavers** together, always hold hands, like this:

In this piece Charly & Quilly run after each other to meet Granpa.
Play all Quilly's Quavers *evenly.*

Charly Crotchet & Quilly Quaver

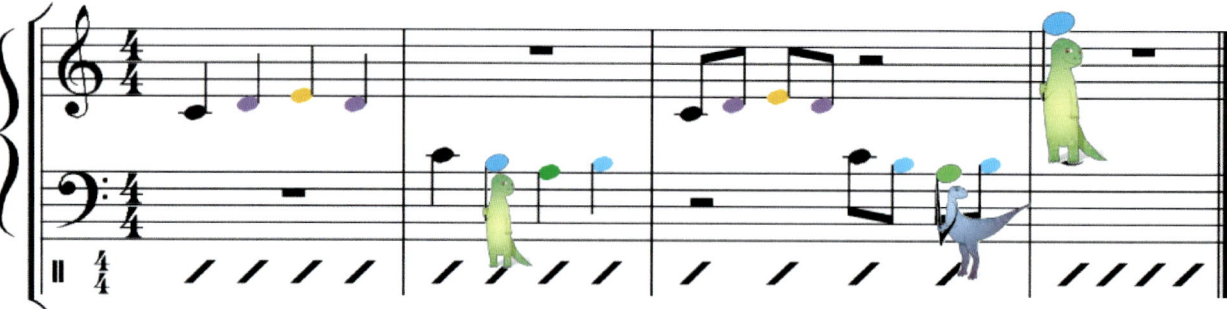

And here's another one you may know ...

Nick Nack Paddywhack

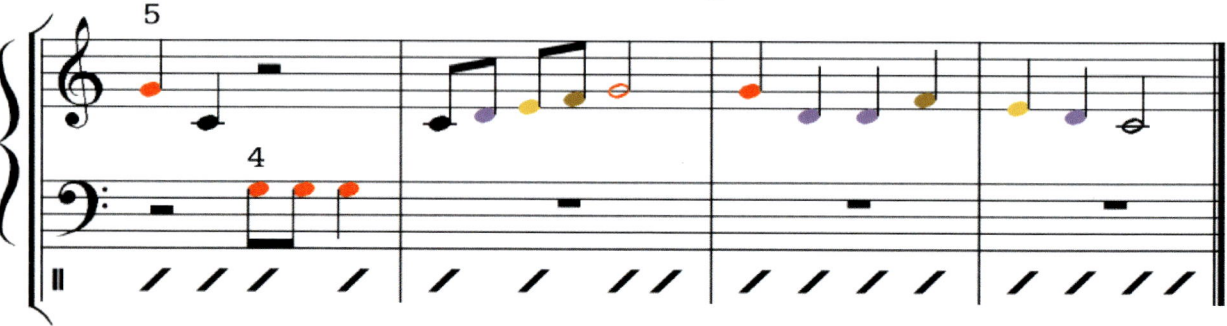

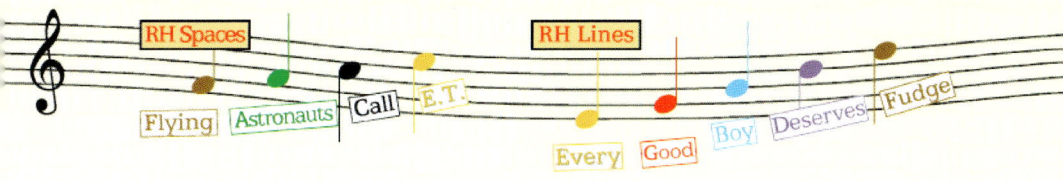

9 London's Burning

Some things before we start ...
    Remember what crotchet rests look like?
    Look: **quavers** can be written _separately_ or _joined up_, but you still play them <u>evenly</u>.
Before you start clap the rhythm Lon- don's burn-ing
                                      Quick Quick Slow Slow

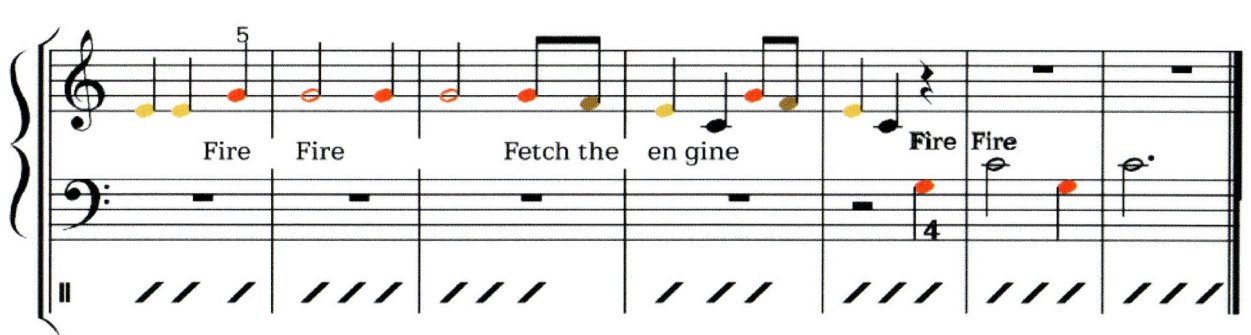

9b Lavender's Blue

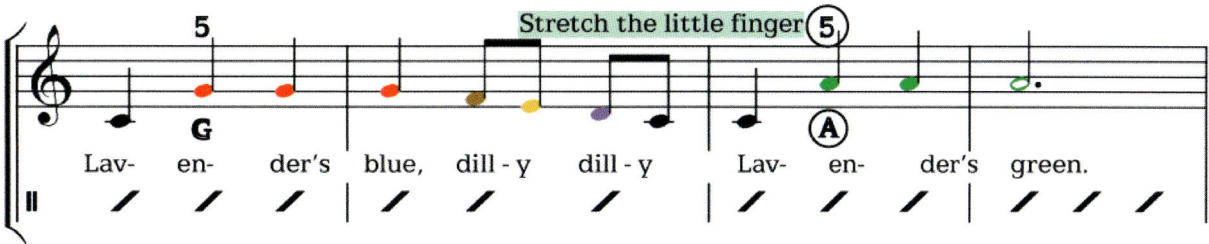

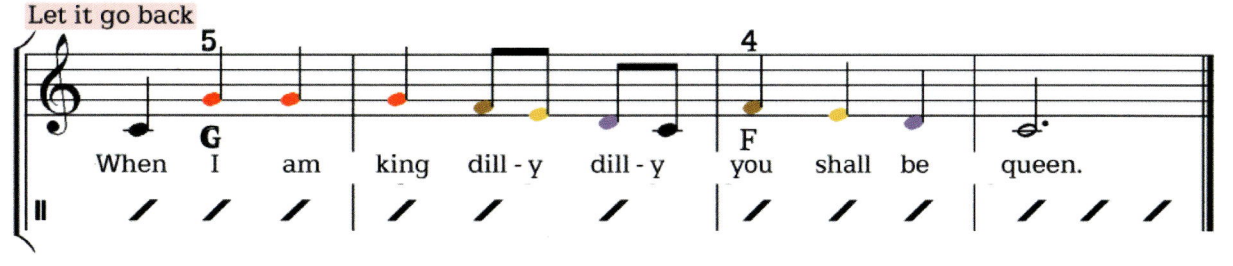

Rests

Semi-breve
4 beats
submarine

Dotted Minim
3 beats

Minim
2 beats
motor boat

dotted Crotchet
1½ beats

Crotchet
1 beat

Quaver
½ beat

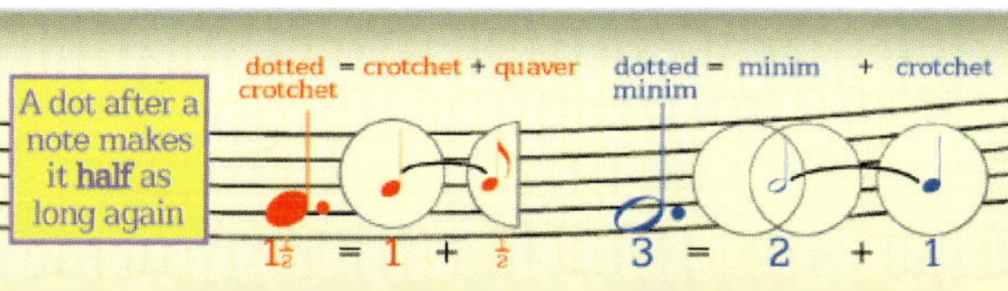

21

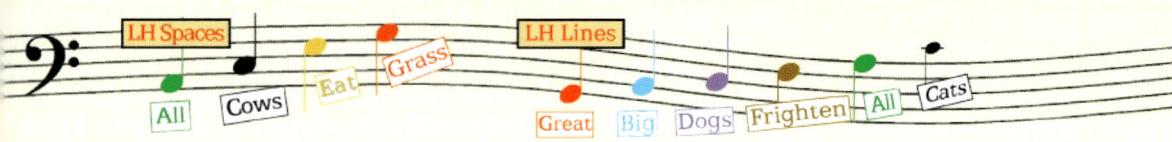

Notes

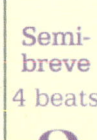
Semi-breve
4 beats

dotted Minim
3 beats

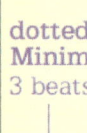
Minim
2 beats

Crotchet
1 beat

Quaver
½ beat

10 Shanty's C Shanty

Vere Harmsworth

10/7/03 age 8

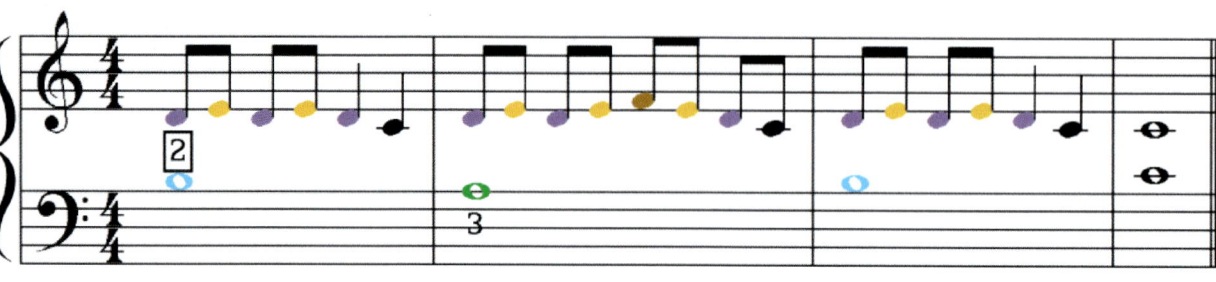

10b 2 Octaves of C major

To play an extra octave (8 notes), you simply go up to the <u>7th note</u> then start again with your thumb.

Count **2 beats** on each key note, *ie*, each C.

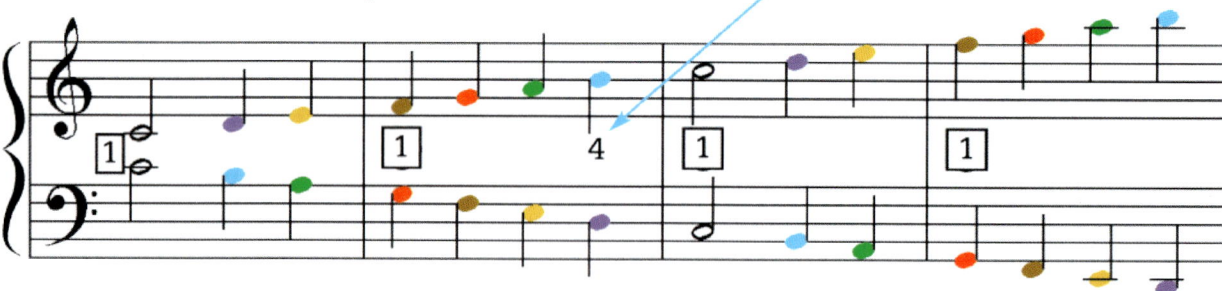

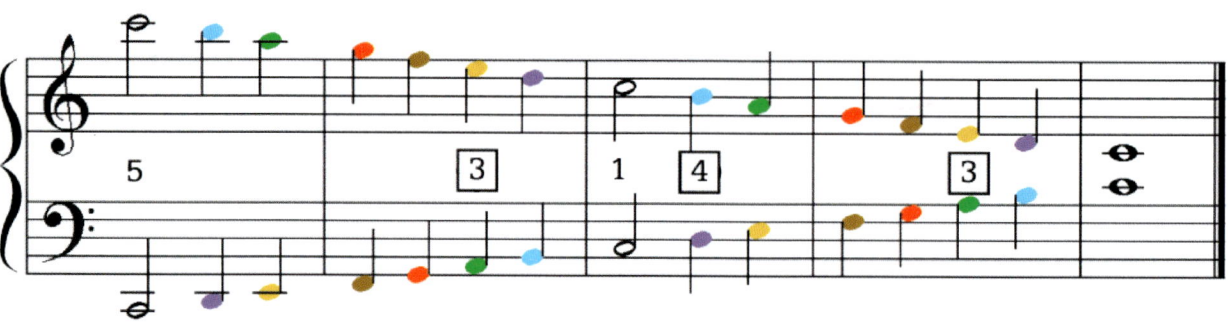

Keep practising this scale until you get to page 24.

Notes

Semi-breve
4 beats

dotted Minim
3 beats

Minim
2 beats

Crotchet
1 beat

Quaver
½ beat

12 A minor Piece

The LH moves up higher – here its top note is yellow E, which is another way of writing the bottom line of the RH Lollipop clef. The extra lines are called 'ledger' lines

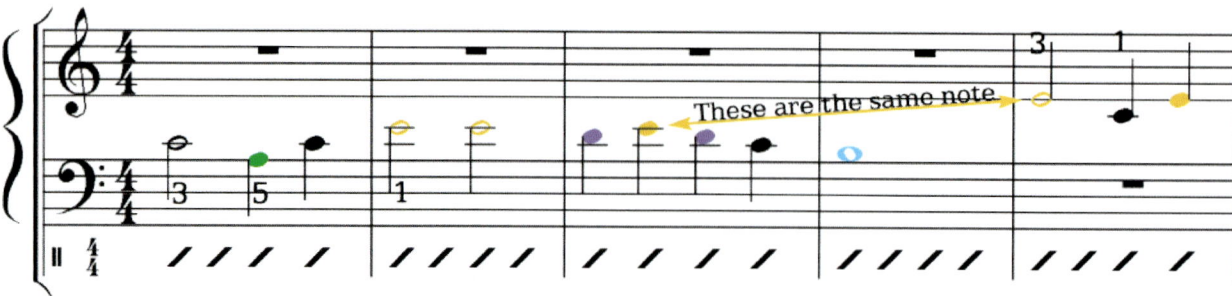

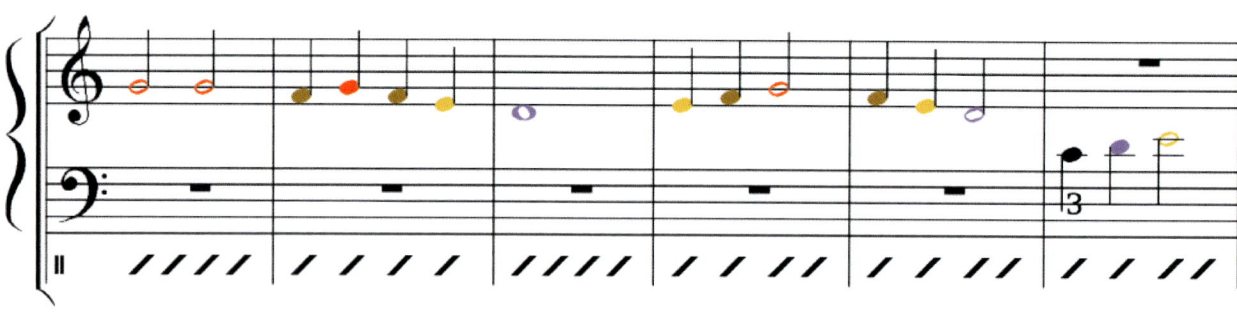

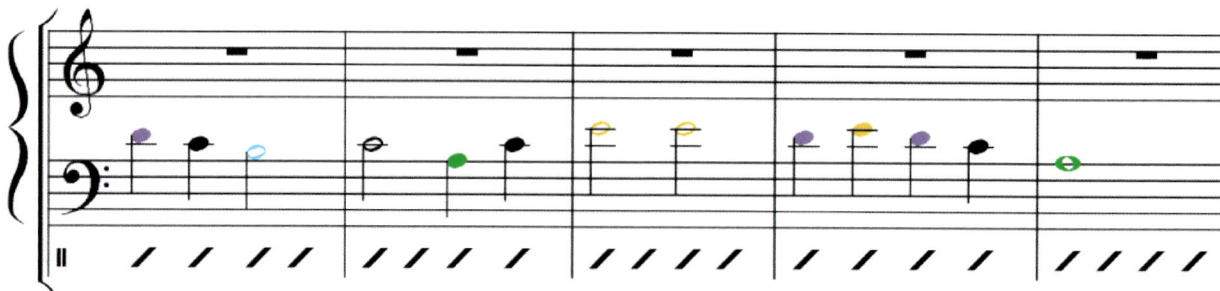

In Tune 13 we see what happens when Charly & Quilly join together. They make a make a skipping rhythm – like dancing around the room.

Say and clap: *Hópp-it-y, Skípp-it-y. Hópp-it-y, Skípp-it-y.*
Look at how the rhythm's written
Make sure that the first note hangs rights over the second beat. Try it counting, but keep the second beat silent, like this:

    1 (/ 2) / 3   1 (/ 2) / 3
    Hóp- it -y,   Skípp- it- y.

13 Skipping

A dot after a note makes it half as long again

Say the words to help you with the rhythm

Rests

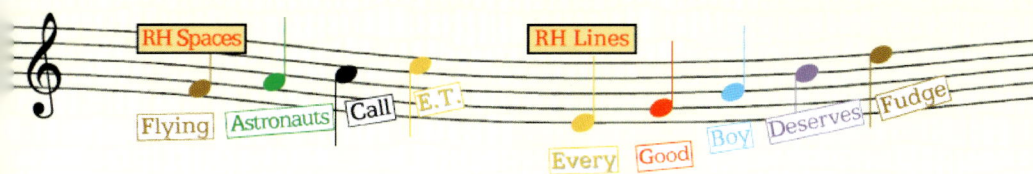

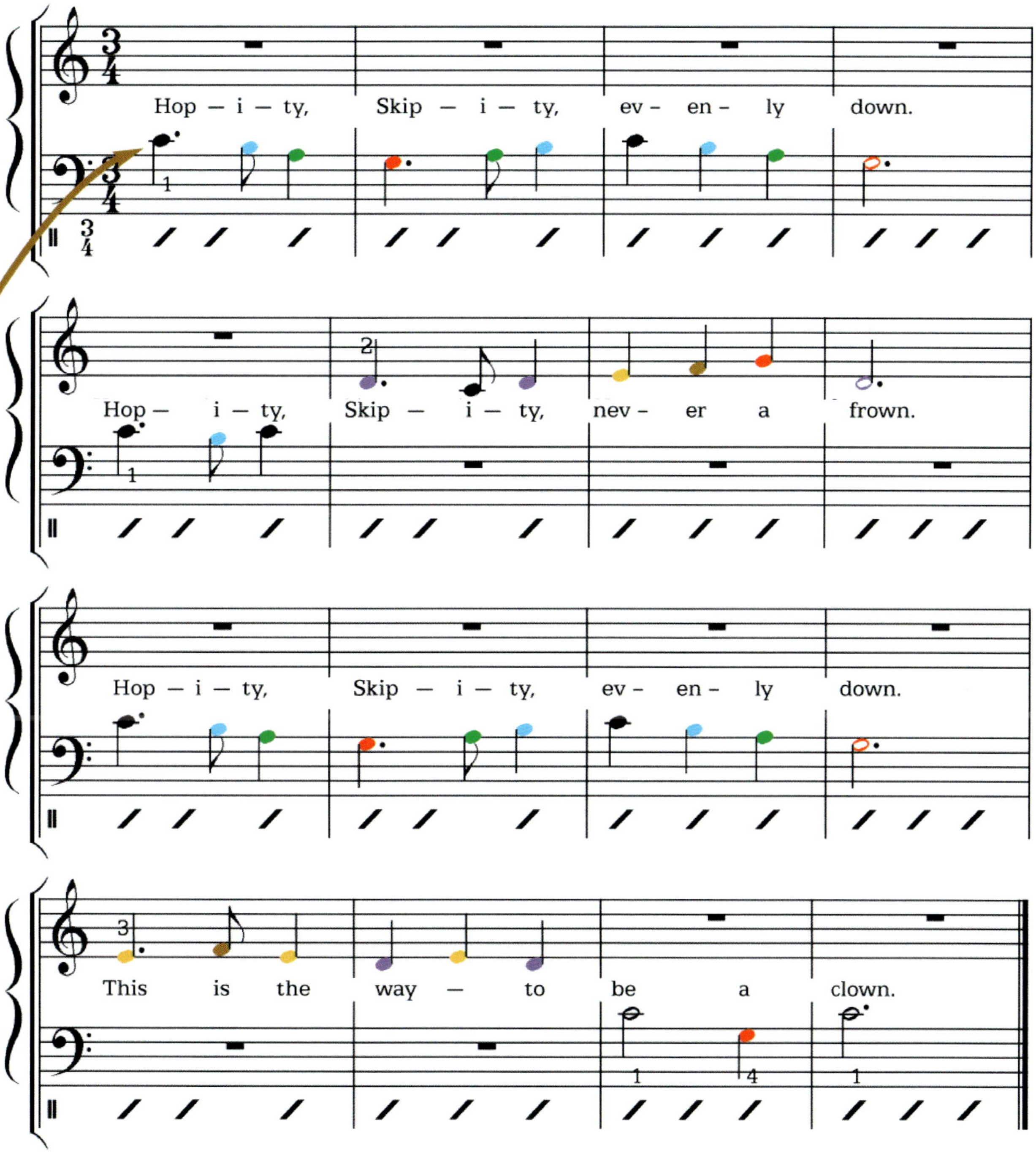

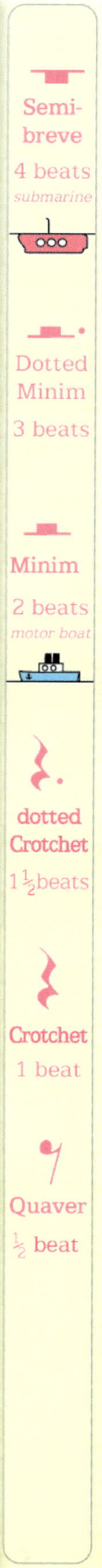

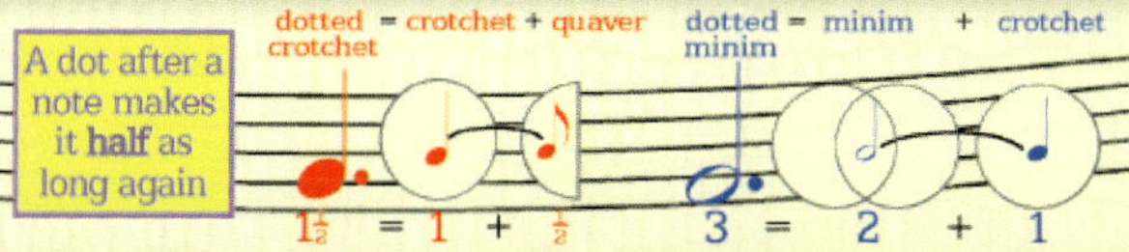

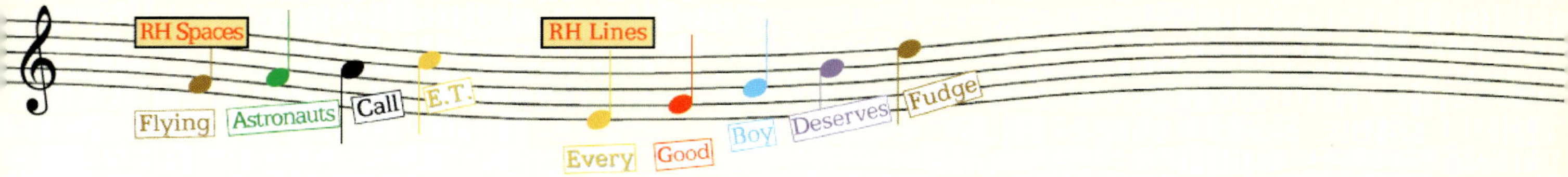

Notes

Semi-breve
4 beats

dotted Minim
3 beats

Minim
2 beats

Crotchet
1 beat

Quaver
½ beat

14 Key Signs & Frère Jacques

So far we haven't used any of the little black keys on the piano.

Black keys don't have their own names. We call them by their nearest white key.

Now we'll use one to play in the key of **G major**. Start on G with your RH thumb and play up using the major scale fingering: 1-2-3—1-2-3-4-5.

You'll notice that to make it sound the same as the C scale you have to play the black key with your fourth finger instead of the normal white key. We call this F# sharp. The sharp sign (#) looks very like the hash key on your phone.

Let's have a look at how that's notated.

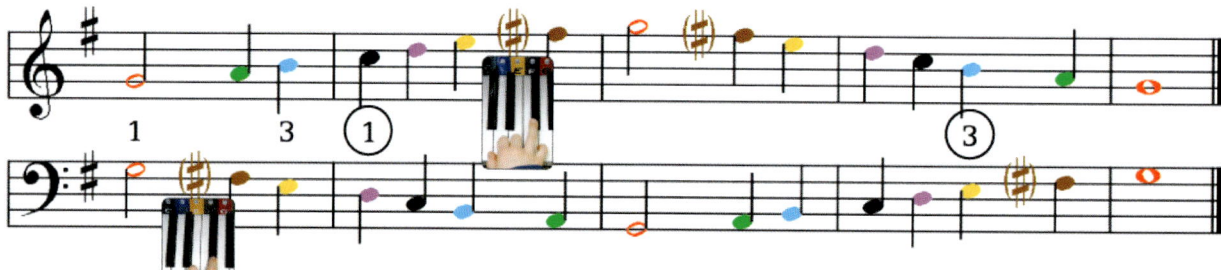

Play each hand separately, and notice how the **F#** comes near the top as you go *up* in the RH: but in the LH it comes as soon as you start down.

It's tricky to play HT as the pattern isn't symmetrical (the same in both hands).

Notice also the sharp written at the beginning. This is what we call a key sign.

It sits at the beginning of each line to remind you that *every* F in the piece *would* be a sharp — however in *Frère Jacques* there actually **aren't** any F#s.

Here you play the same note with different fingers

15 JINGLE BELLS

The tune is simplified to make it easier to play. **Don't start too fast.**
Play lines 1 & 2 first. Notice that the **LH plays the next C down** from Middle C.
Lines 3 & 4 are the same music in G major.

C here is short for **Common** Time, which is 4 beats in a bar, 4/4 time

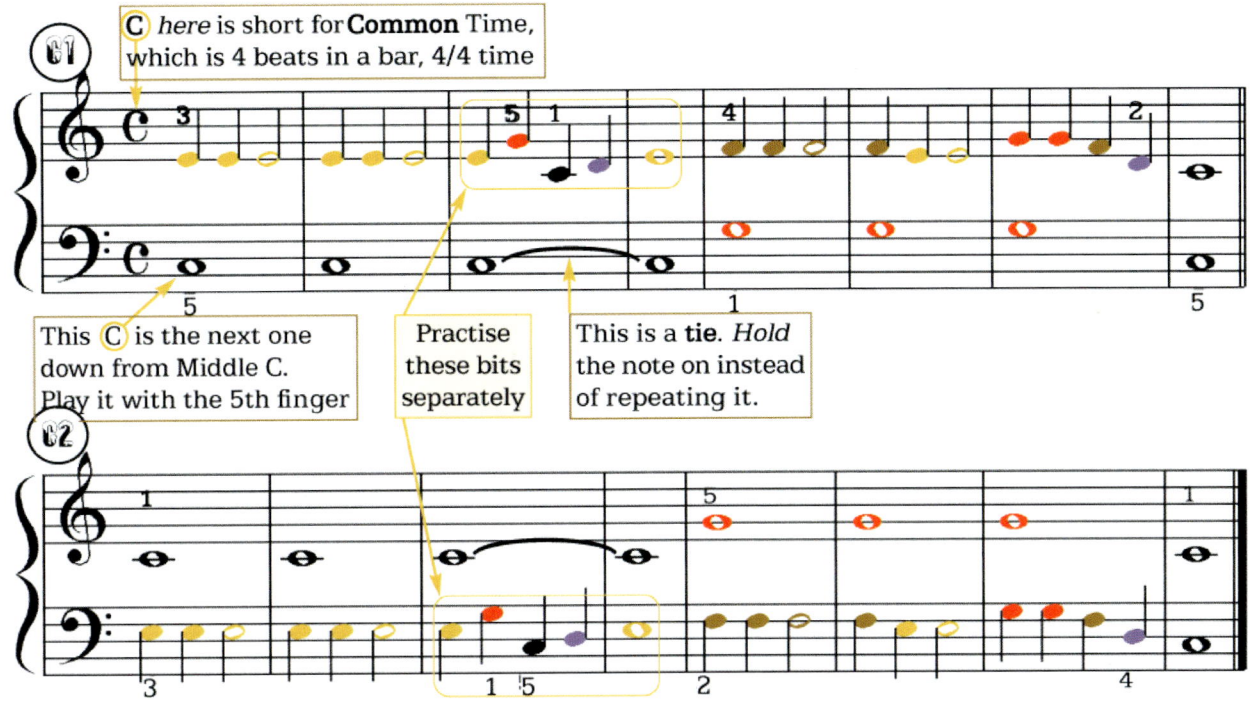

This **C** is the next one down from Middle C. Play it with the 5th finger

Practise these bits separately

This is a **tie.** *Hold the note on instead of repeating it.*

Now play it in G major.
Luckily this piece doesn't use the note F so you don't have to worry about the

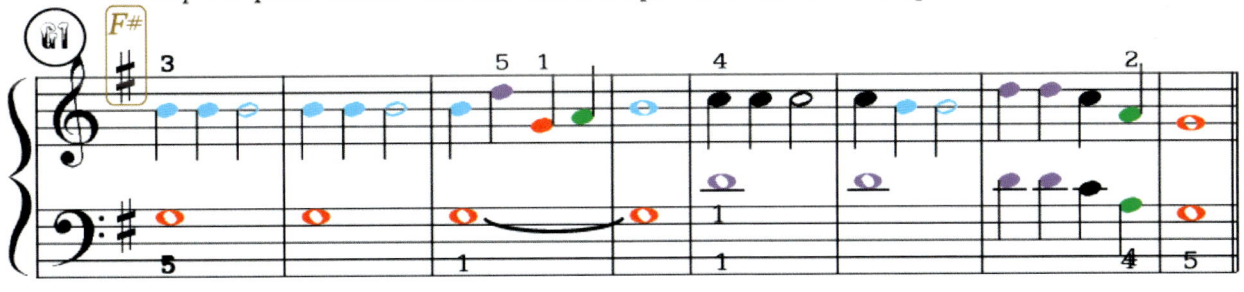

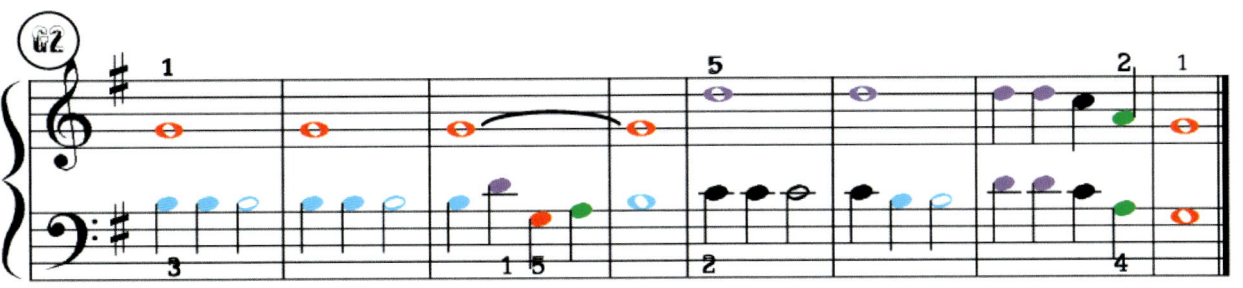

Continue practising G major.
When you feel confident use the two octave version on p43

Rests

Semi-breve
4 beats
submarine

Dotted Minim
3 beats

Minim
2 beats
motor boat

dotted Crotchet
1½ beats

Crotchet
1 beat

Quaver
½ beat

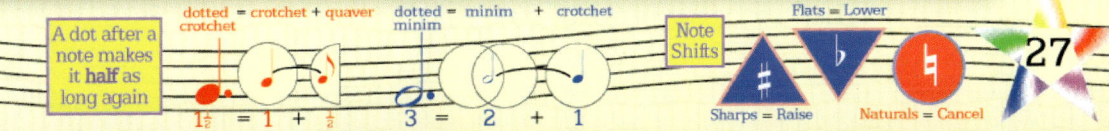

Flats

Remember about the **sharps** (#) telling you to play the next black key *higher*? Well now we meet **flats (b)** telling you to play the next black key **lower**. Like this ...

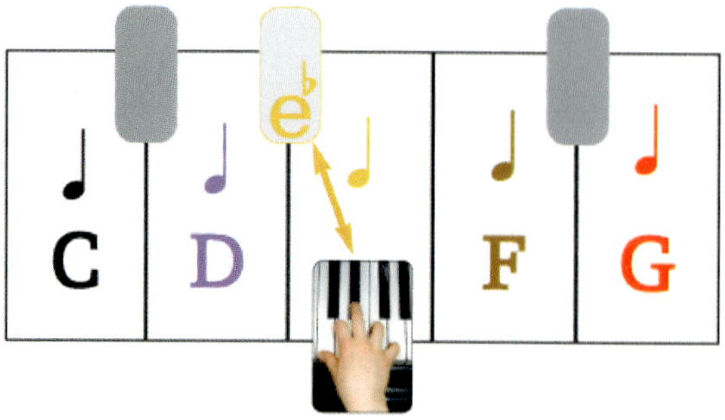

16 Night River

Rushka Moore
21/9/98 aged 11

*The C is tied. **Hold** it on when you play the G*

Here you must stretch the thumb

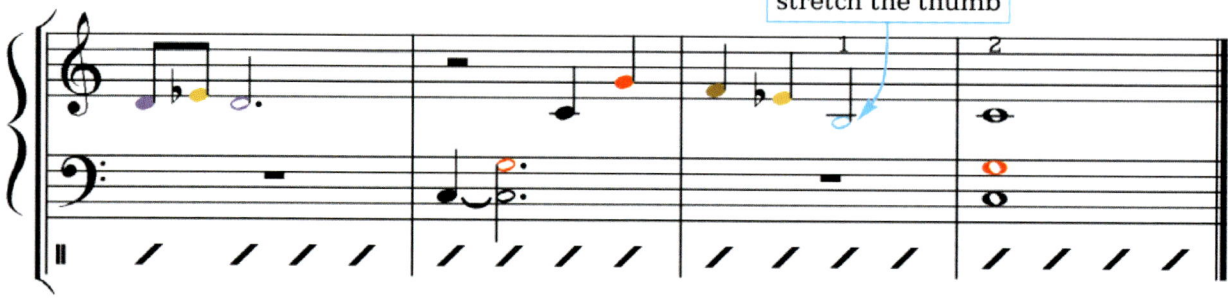

18 Silent Night

Remember #13? Well this is the same skipping rhythm again.
Here are our friends to remind us that **a dot after a note makes it half as long again.** Use the grid to help you count (This is the last time we'll use it.)

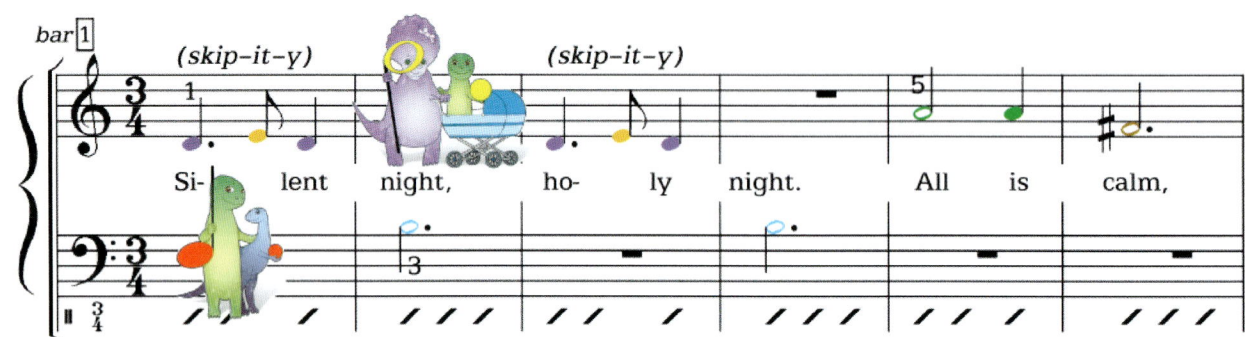

Si- lent night, ho- ly night. All is calm,

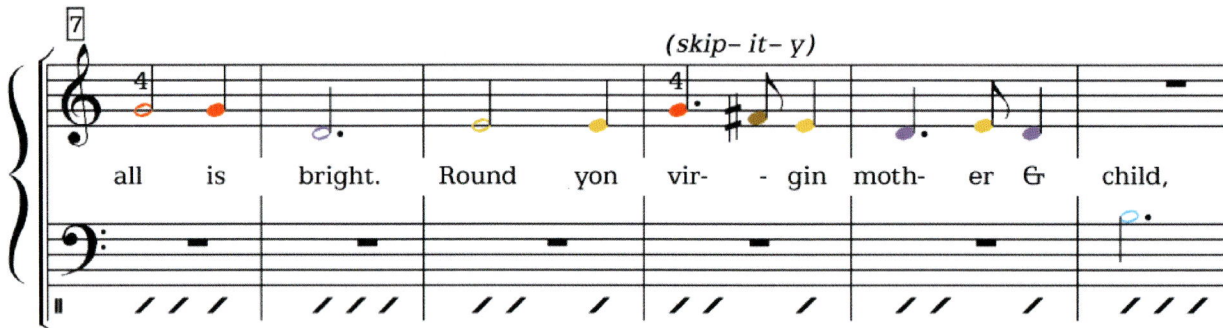

all is bright. Round yon vir- gin moth- er & child,

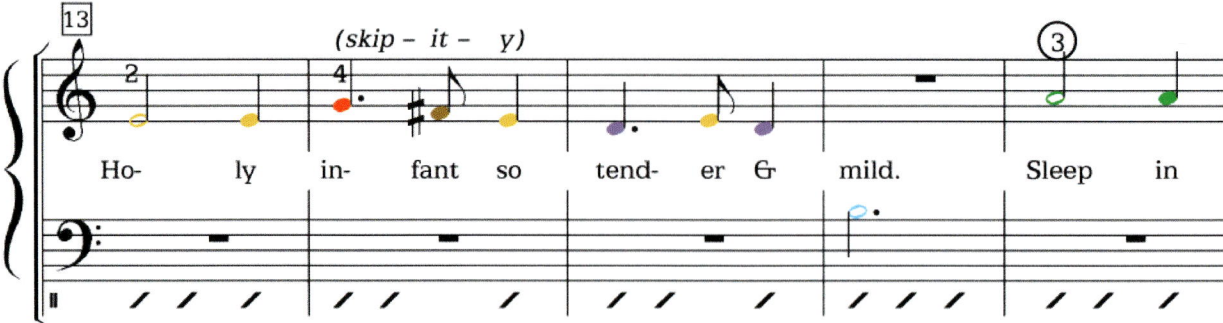

Ho- ly in- fant so tend- er & mild. Sleep in

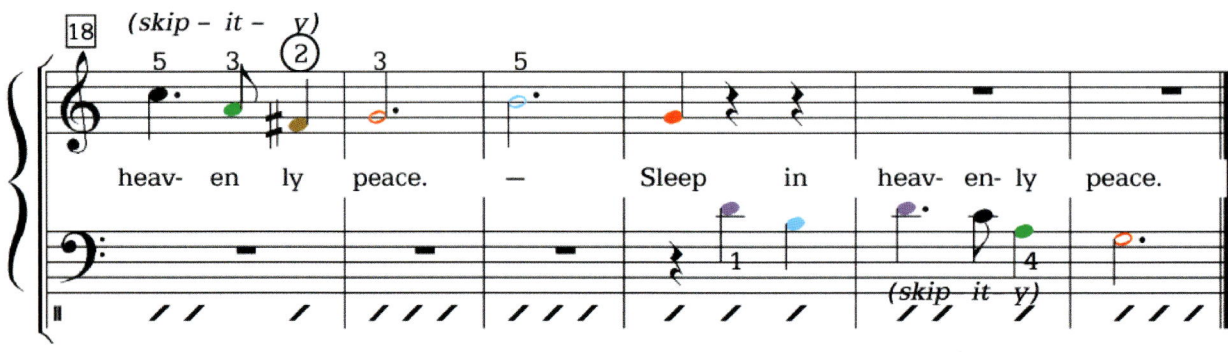

heav- en- ly peace. — Sleep in heav- en- ly peace.

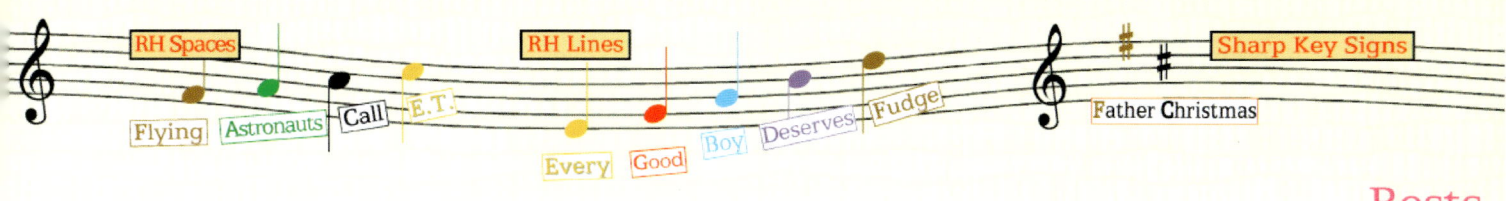

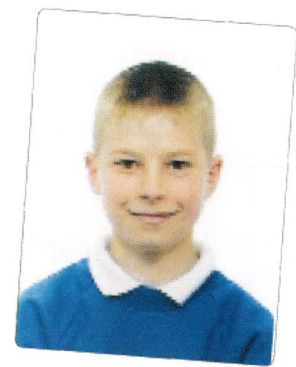

19a Just Bit

Matthew McTigue

9/10/02 age 12.

Play Wait & Run & Stop

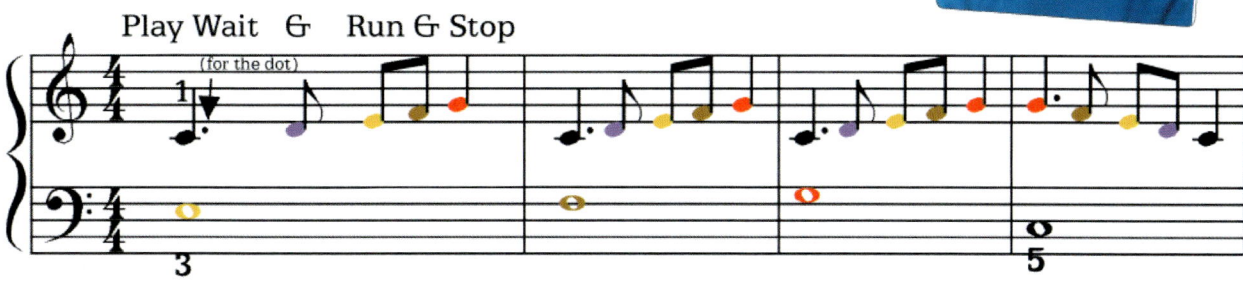

19b The Long & Short of It

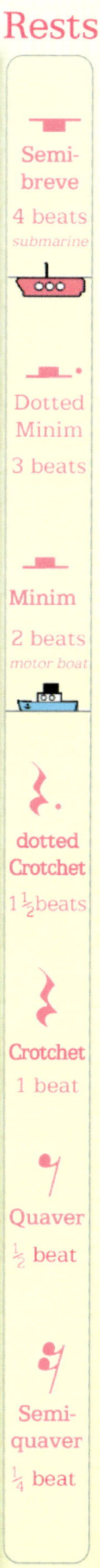

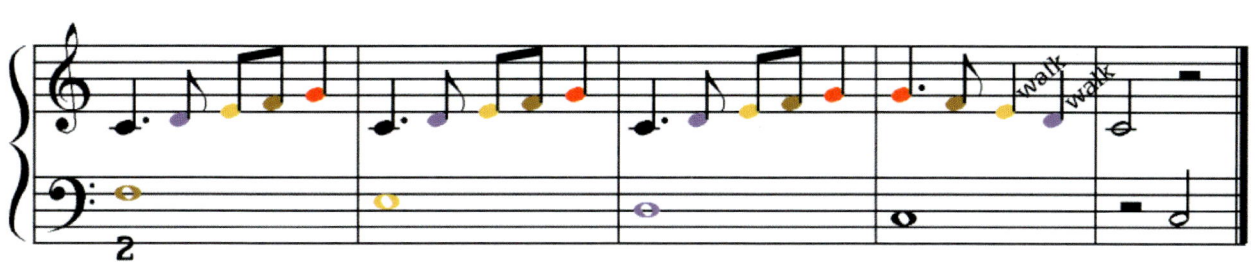

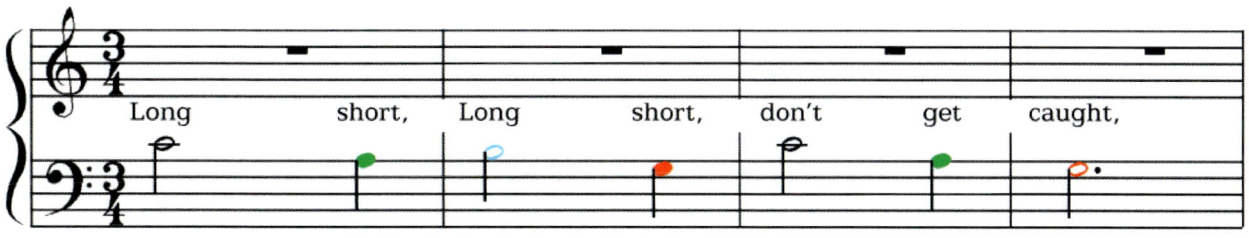

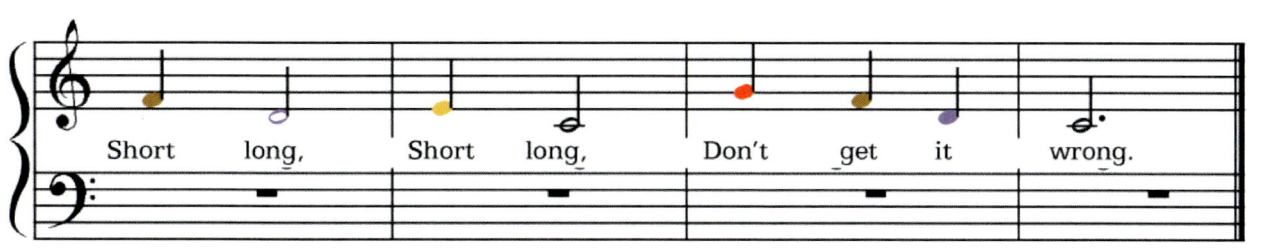

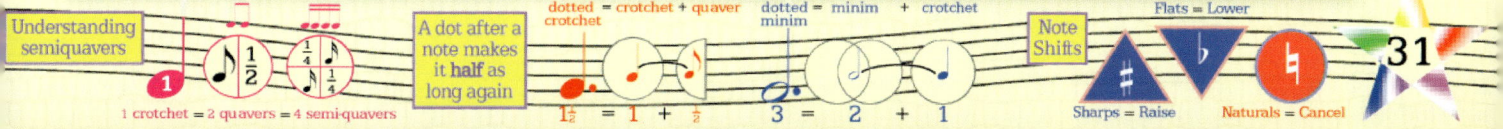

Notes

20a The First

Josh Chaloner

22/03/03 age 9

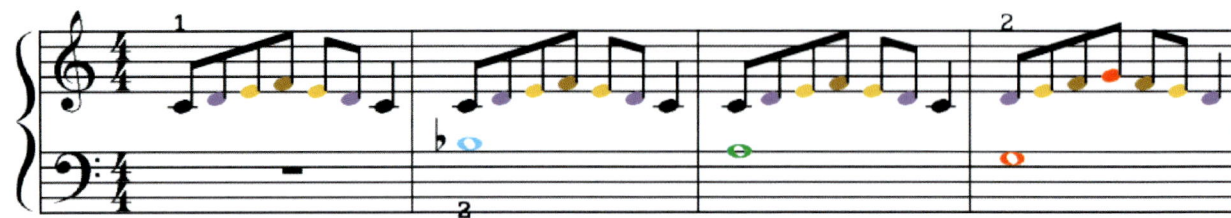

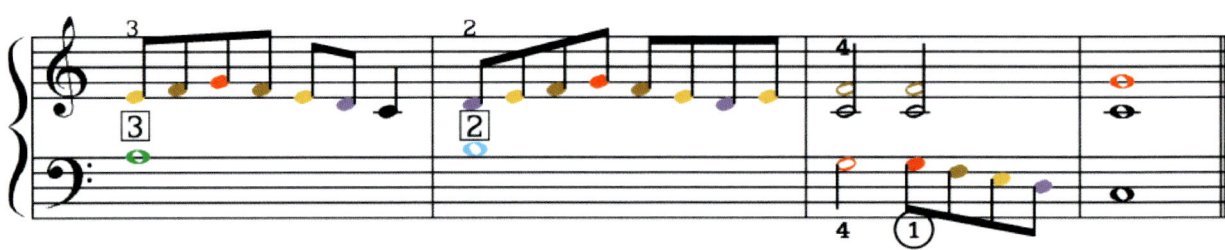

20b Barcarolle

Jacques Offenbach

See what you can find out about him on the web

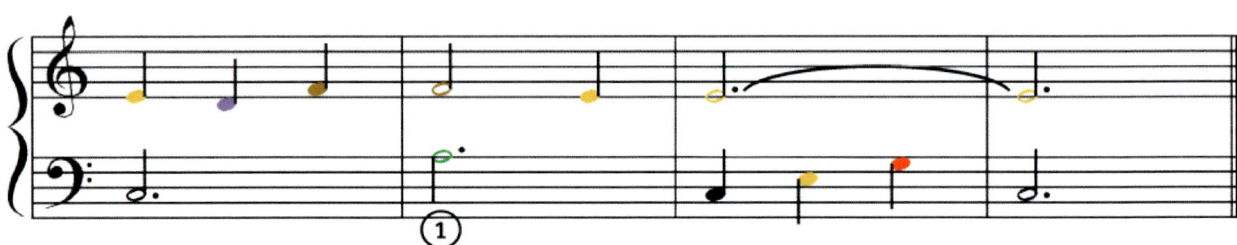

If you've been getting on ok with G major scale, try D major now – see p43.

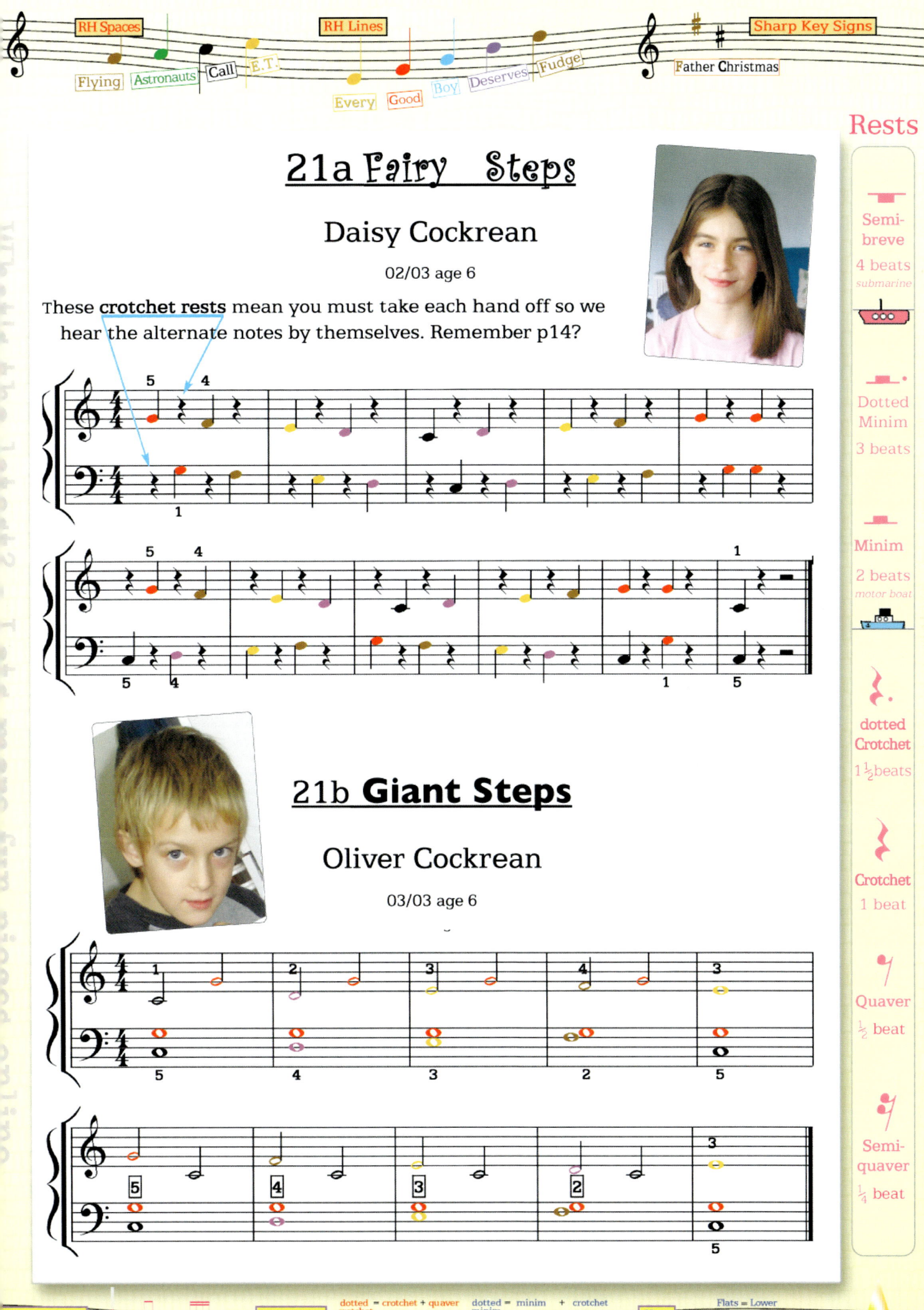

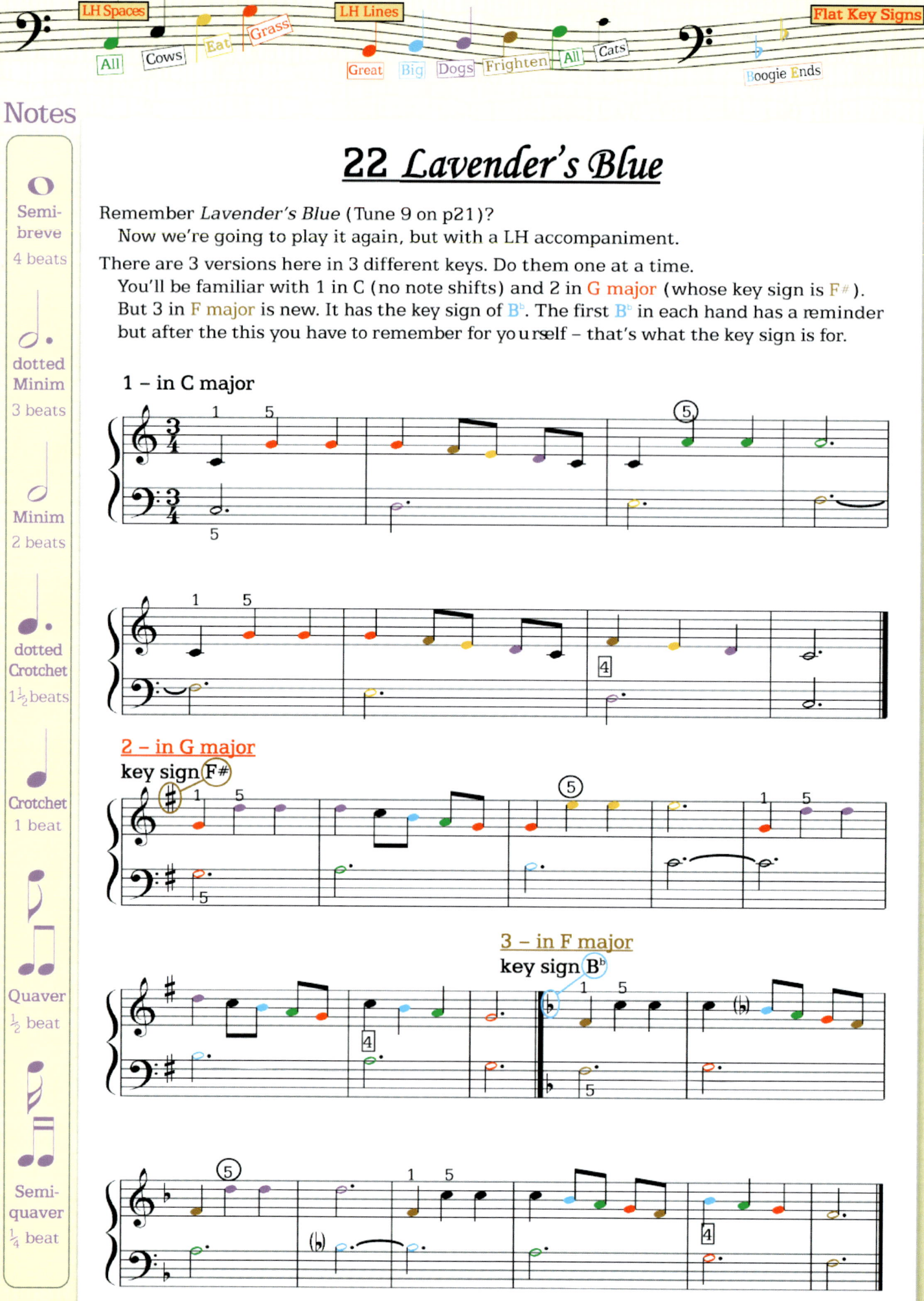

23 CAN U.B. SURE?

Simon Mudd

12/97 age 8

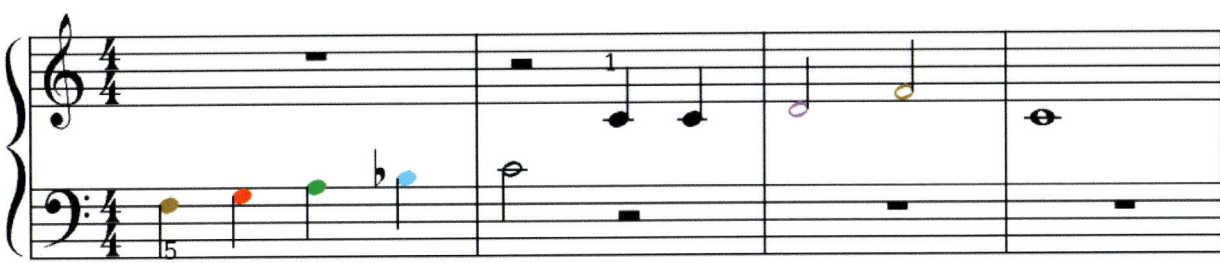
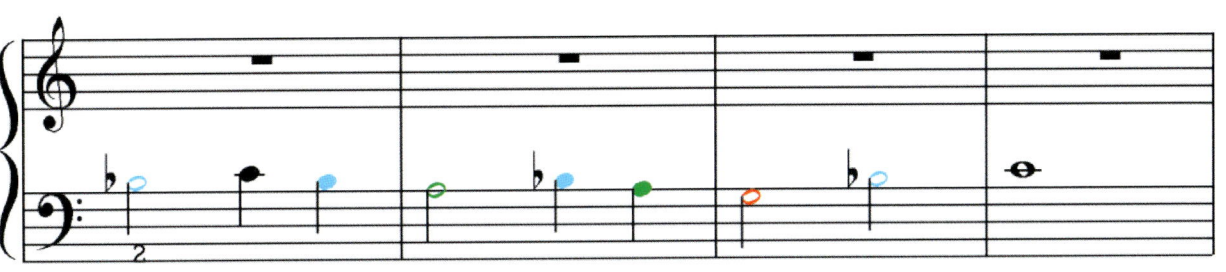
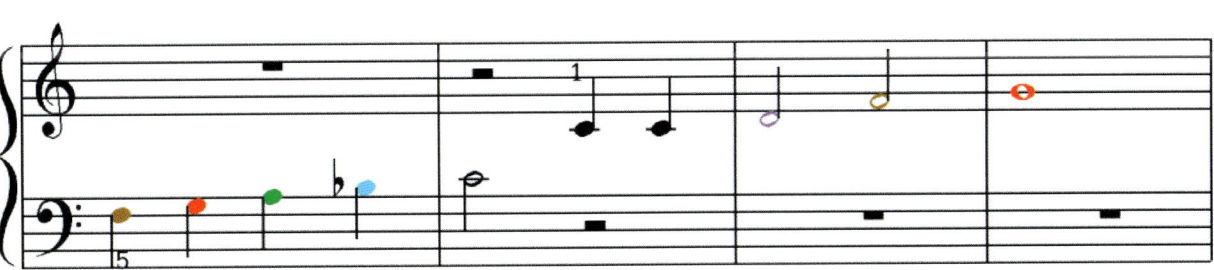

Here the RH jumps to a higher position

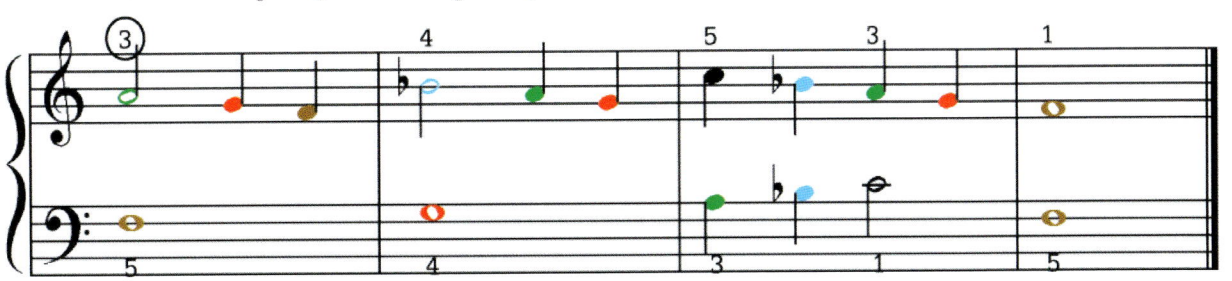
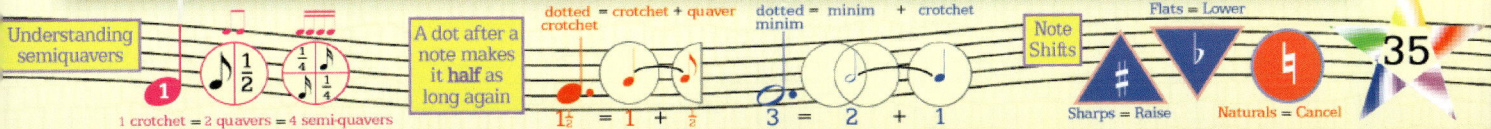

Notes

- **Semibreve** — 4 beats ○
- **dotted Minim** — 3 beats
- **Minim** — 2 beats
- **dotted Crotchet** — 1½ beats
- **Crotchet** — 1 beat
- **Quaver** — ½ beat
- **Semiquaver** — ¼ beat

24 BOOGIE

Play the first line by itself. Use the words to help you get the rhythm. – then clap and play the 'go & bounce the 4th fing-' remembering to *bounce* the '4th fing' twice!
Play the 2nd line separately so that you're clear about how it's different.

Next, practise lines 3 & 4 by themselves. Now we have to practise moving both hands up at the end of line 3, and down at the end of line 4.
At the end of line 2 you finish on the 4th finger. Swop it for both your thumbs & then you're in position to play line 3. At the end do the maneuver in reverse.
The hard part is that you've got to do it in 4 beats - but you'll manage it with practise!

The dots **over** or **under** notes mean you play them short. It's called *staccato*.
(Don't confuse this with dots **after** notes which mean you hold them on half as long again.)

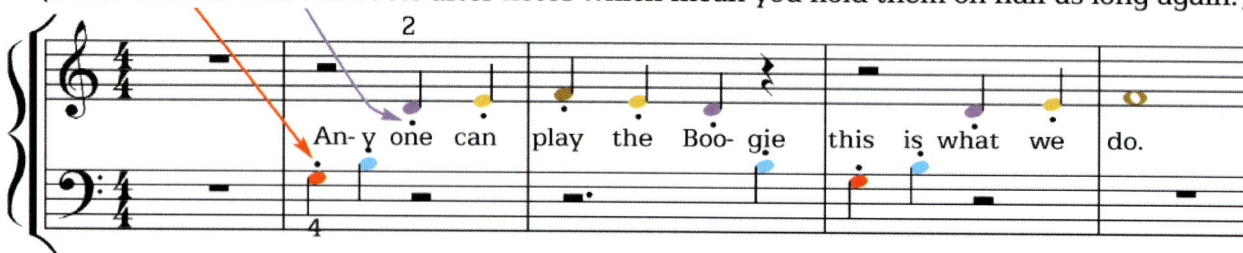

An-y one can play the Boo-gie this is what we do.

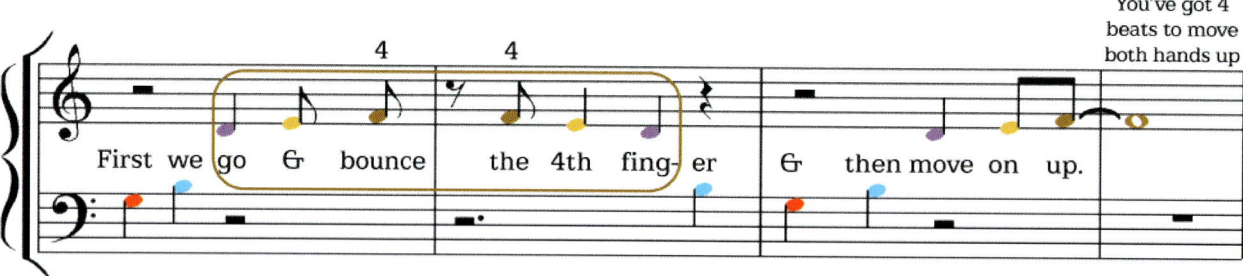

First we go & bounce the 4th fing-er & then move on up.

You've got 4 beats to move both hands up

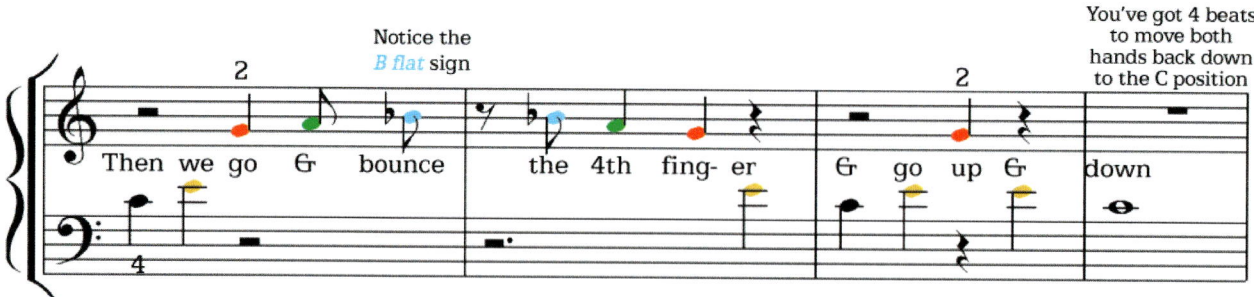

Then we go & bounce the 4th fing-er & go up & down

Notice the *B flat* sign

You've got 4 beats to move both hands back down to the C position

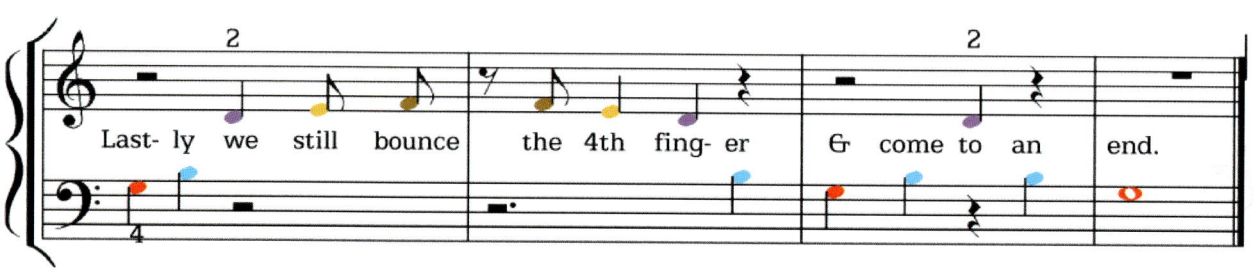

Last-ly we still bounce the 4th fing-er & come to an end.

BOOGIE ACCOMPANIMENT

This accompaniment is on the CD.
But if someone can play it, so much the better.
If the soloist is a young person, an adult can reach around their back & play either side of them!

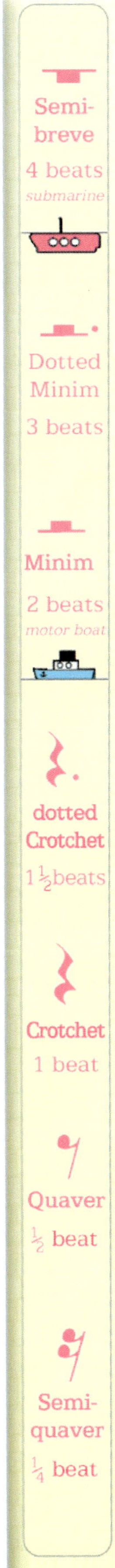

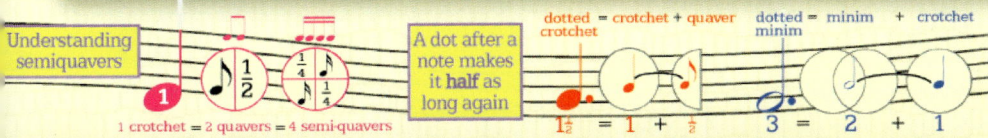

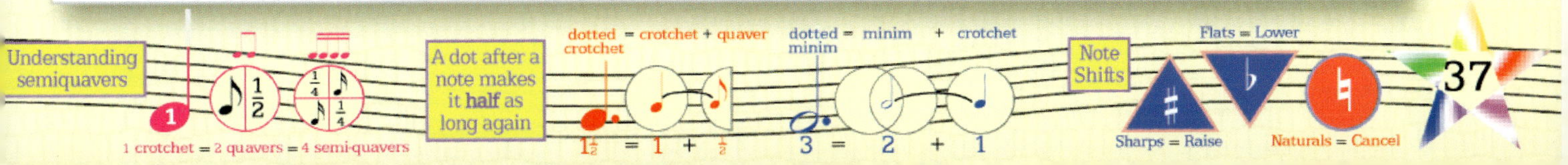

Notes

○ Semi-breve 4 beats

𝅗𝅥. dotted Minim 3 beats

𝅗𝅥 Minim 2 beats

𝅘𝅥. dotted Crotchet 1½ beats

𝅘𝅥 Crotchet 1 beat

𝅘𝅥𝅮 Quaver ½ beat

𝅘𝅥𝅯 Semi-quaver ¼ beat

25 The Circuit

This is a well-known doodle. It makes a fun duet – especially if you play it all twice, Notice the rhythm "I'd like a cup of tea" with the dotted quaver & the semiquaver. Use the chart at the side of the page to work it out. The notes can be written separately or joined together – notice how the semiquaver is written when it's joined to a dotted quaver.

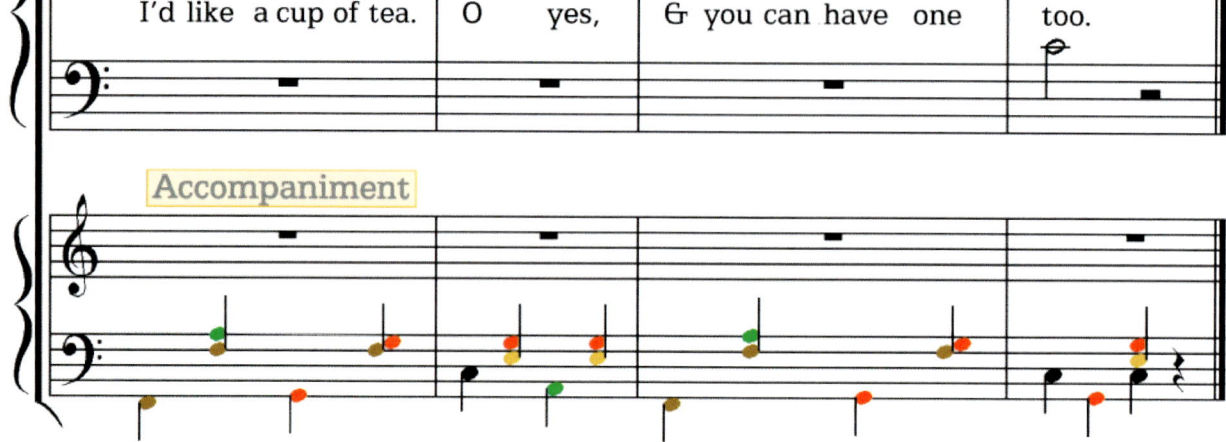

38

26 Horseriding

Matthew Wilkins

22/03/03

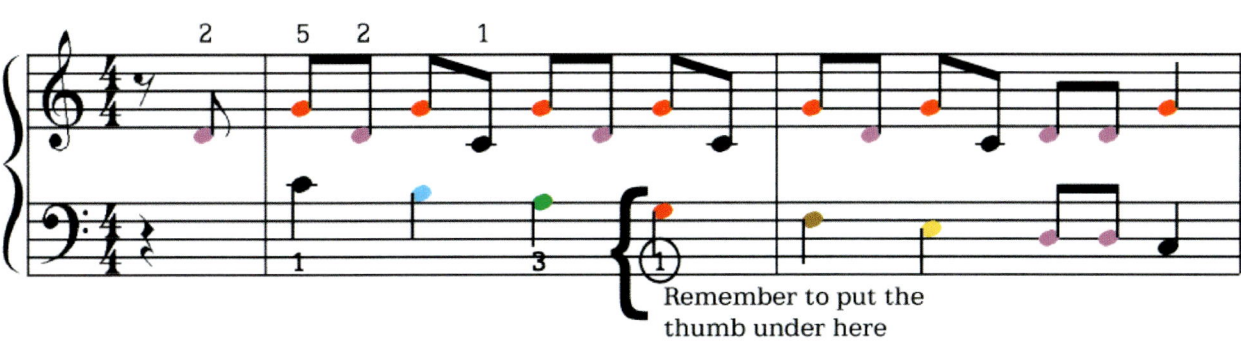

Remember to put the thumb under here

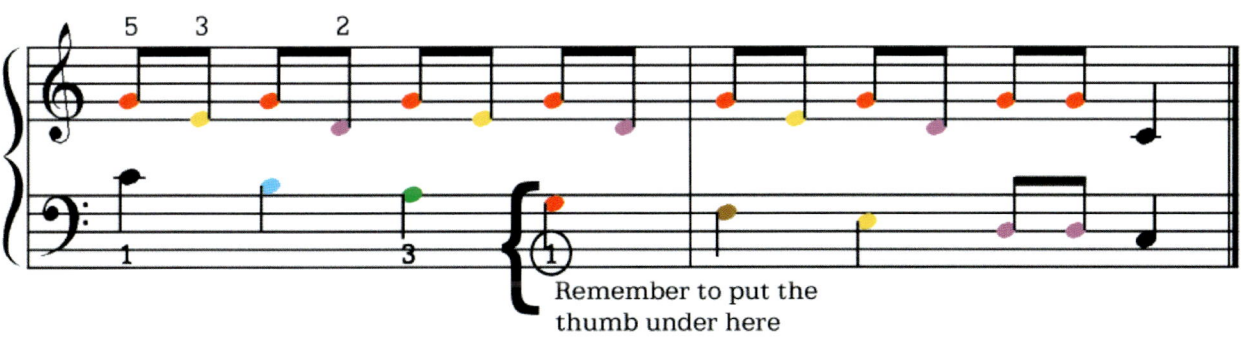

Remember to put the thumb under here

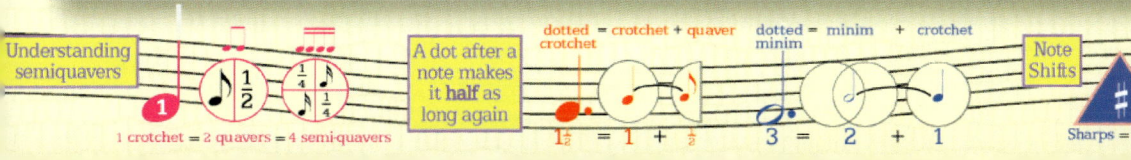

27 The Ashgrove

This beautiful old Irish tune has a couple of difficult moments. To perfect it start with the quavers in box I to get them fast & even, beginning with the 5th finger.

Next tackle the quavers in box II the same way, bearing in mind that you begin on the 4th finger & end by putting the 2nd over.

Lastly, play it all without box III. Once you're confident about the timing, add that bit in too.

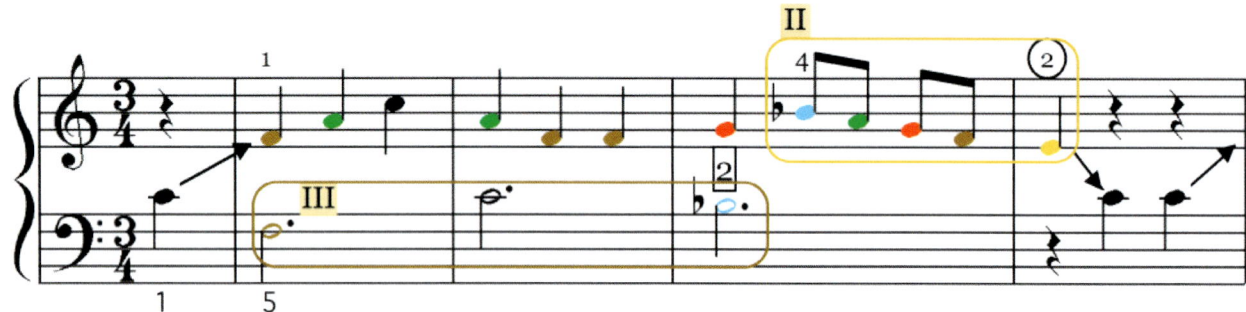

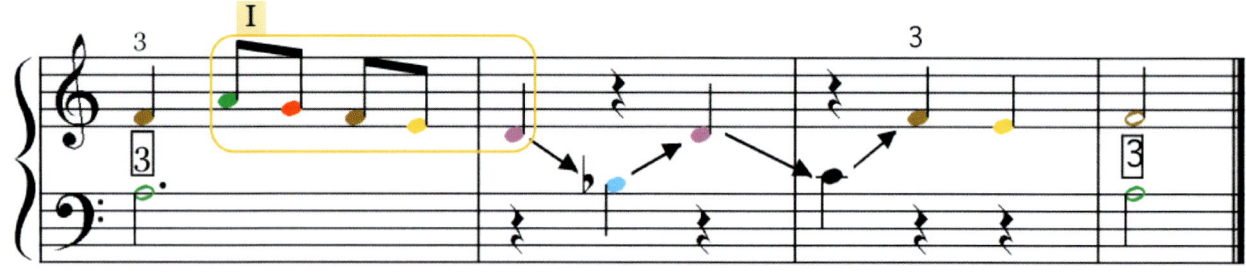

28 Double Decker

Finn Murphy

11/01/06 age 7

This piece gives you a chance to practise playing the same chord on next-door notes. Make sure you're confident playing it H/S before putting H/T.

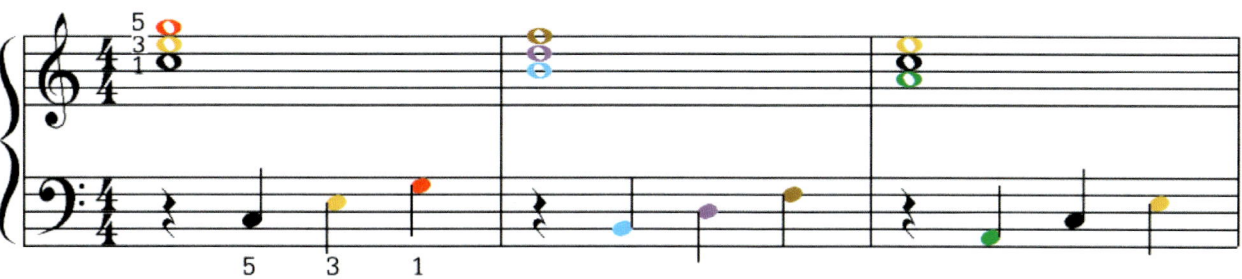

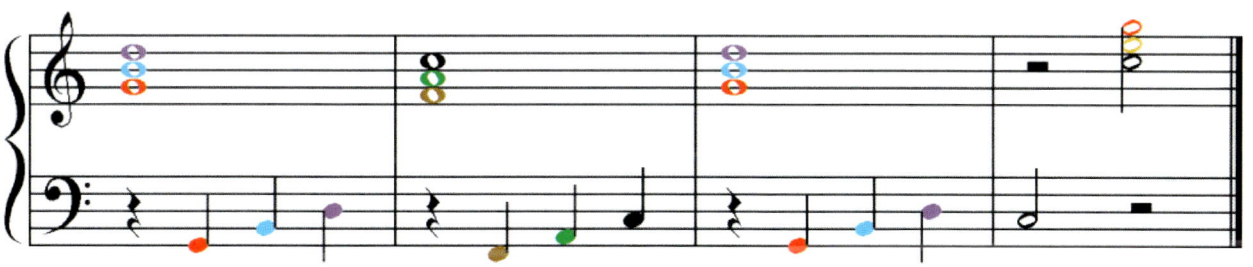

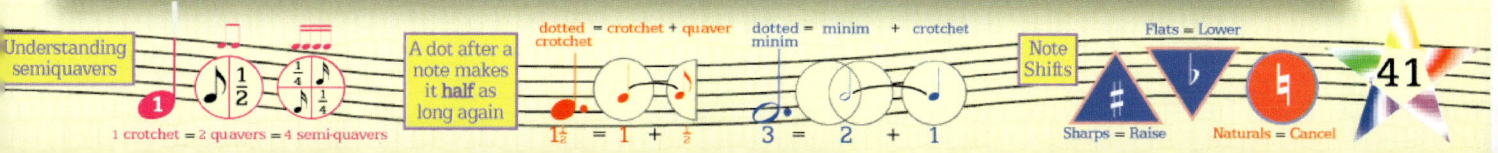

Notes

○ Semi-breve 4 beats

𝅗𝅥. dotted Minim 3 beats

𝅗𝅥 Minim 2 beats

𝅘𝅥. dotted Crotchet 1½ beats

𝅘𝅥 Crotchet 1 beat

𝅘𝅥𝅮 Quaver ½ beat

𝅘𝅥𝅯 Semi-quaver ¼ beat

29 Happy Birthday 2 U

In the first line the hands mostly mirror each other.

In the second line the LH jumps an octave (8 notes from G–G).

After that all the notes are next door to each other.

See that the semiquavers are really crisp

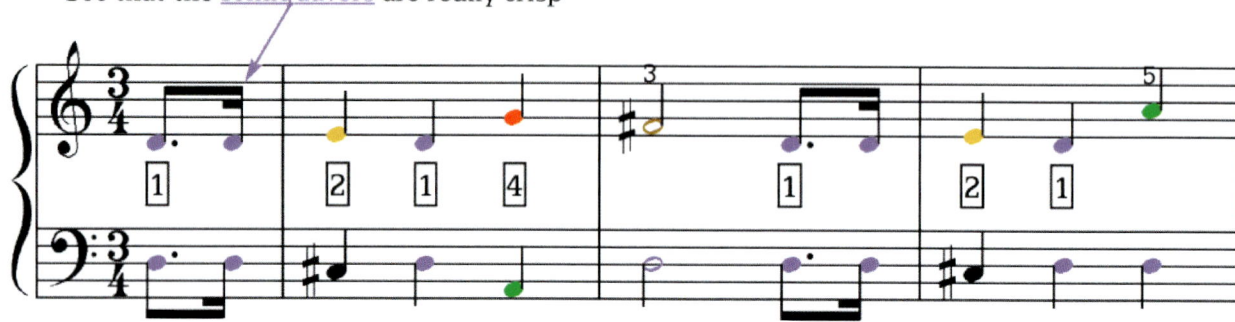

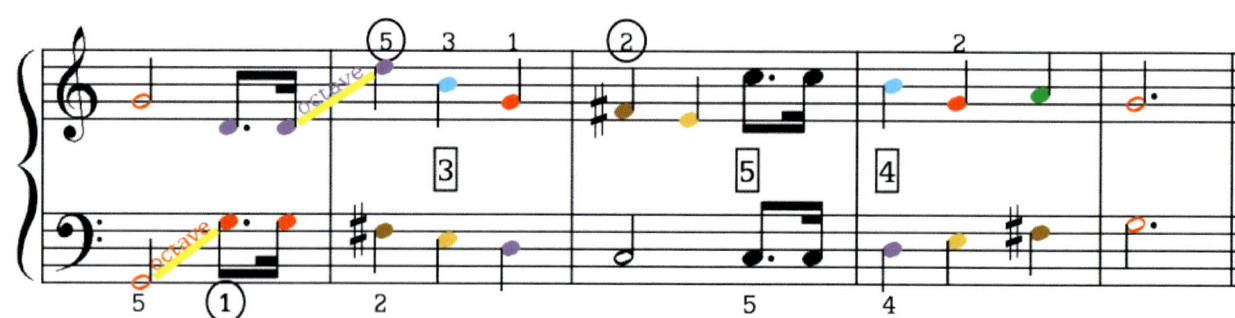

An octave is when you jump from any note to the next one of the same colour.

42 Time Signs 4/4 or C = 𝅘𝅥 𝅘𝅥 𝅘𝅥 𝅘𝅥   3/4 = 𝅘𝅥 𝅘𝅥 𝅘𝅥   2/4 = 𝅘𝅥 𝅘𝅥

ColourMuse

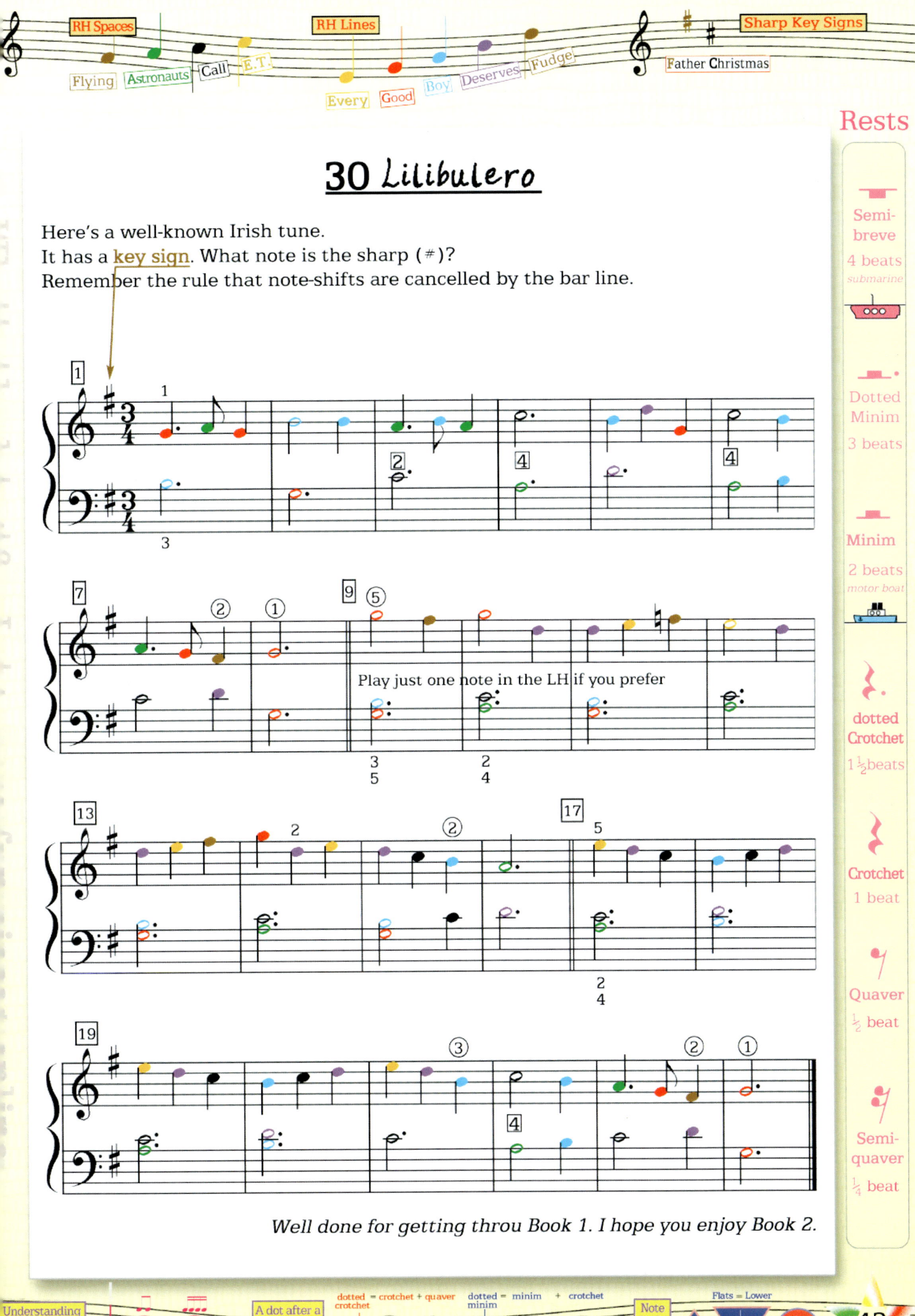

Scales

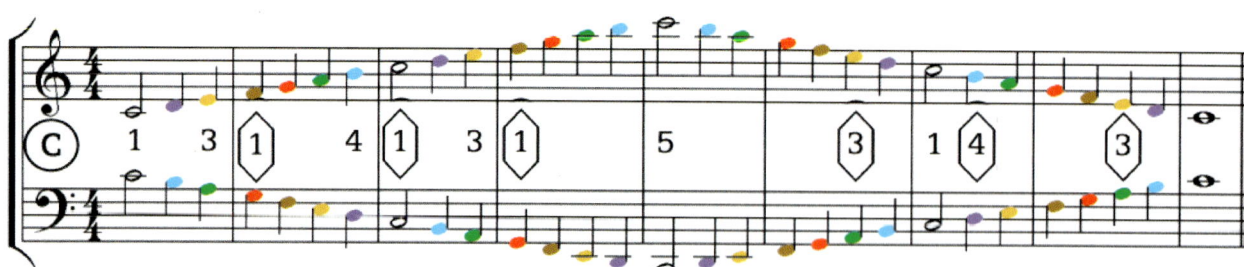

F# (Father)

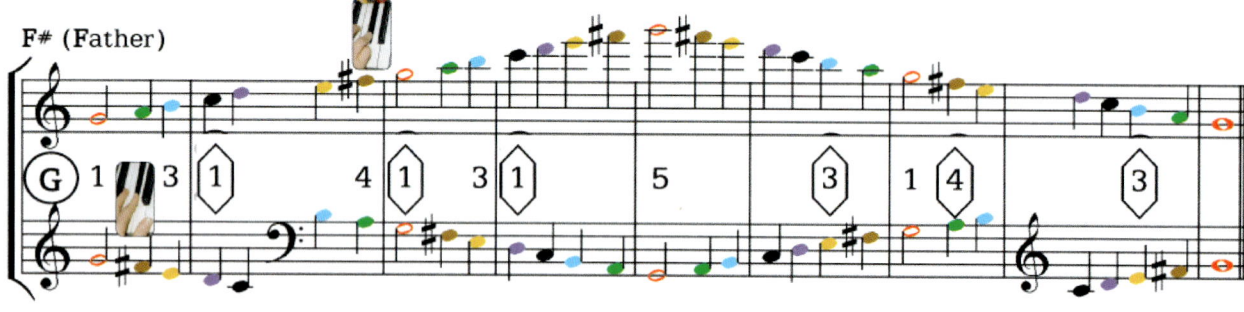

Going up, each LH# (sharp) is followed directly by a RH# *Going down* it's the opposite
F# C# (Father Christmas)

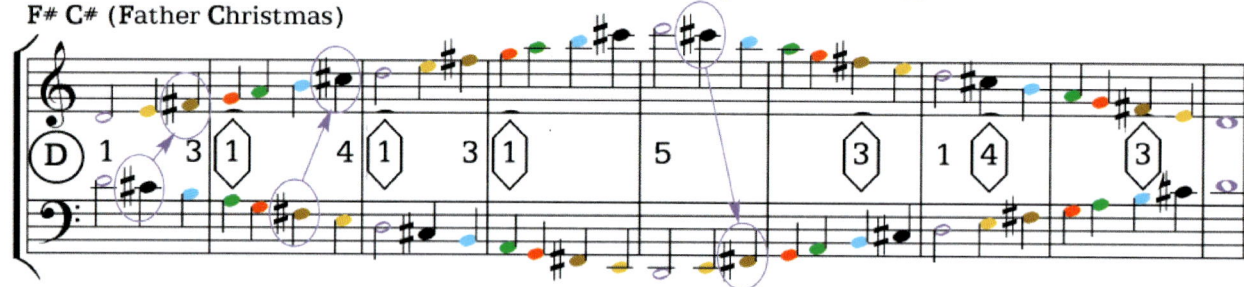

In A major both **3**rd fingers are always on black keys together
F# C# G# (Father Christmas Gets)

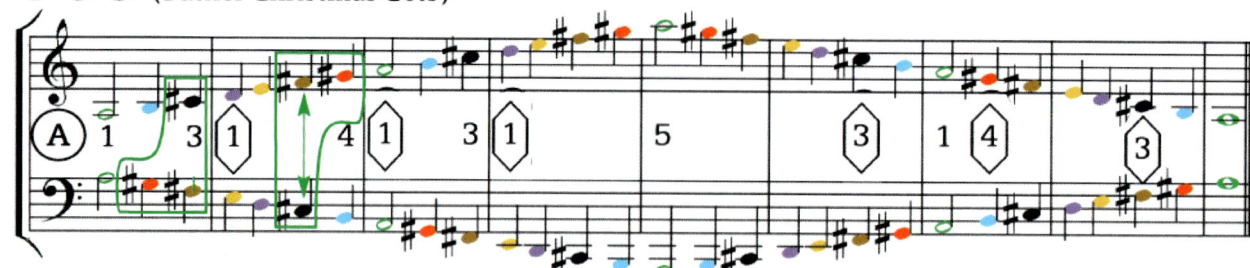

In E major all the ## are symmetrical.
The pattern is **E**, black black, white white, black black, **E**
F# C# G# D# (Father Christmas Gets Down)

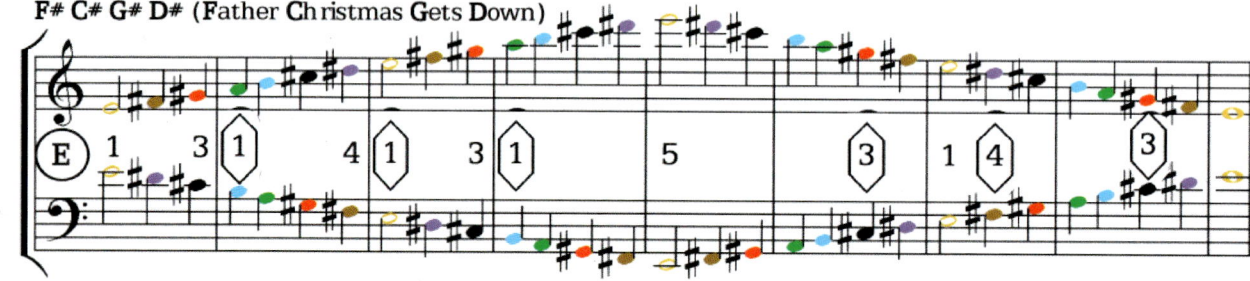